THE PRESIDENT AND ME:

★ ★ ★ ★ ★ ★ ★

Thomas Jefferson

AND THE RETURN OF THE MAGIC HAT

DEBORAH KALB

Schiffer **Kids**™

4880 Lower Valley Road, Atglen, PA 19310

Other Books in the Series:

George Washington and the Magic Hat, ISBN 978-0-7643-5110-5

John Adams and the Magic Bobblehead, ISBN 978-0-7643-5556-1

Cover design by Brenda McCallum
Type set in Bookman Old Style

ISBN: 978-0-7643-6019-0
Printed in China

Published by Schiffer Kids
An imprint of Schiffer Publishing, Ltd.
4880 Lower Valley Road
Atglen, PA 19310
Phone: (610) 593-1777; Fax: (610) 593-2002
E-mail: Info@schifferbooks.com
Web: www.schifferbooks.com

For our complete selection of fine books on this and related subjects, please visit our website at www.schifferbooks.com. You may also write for a free catalog.

Schiffer Publishing's titles are available at special discounts for bulk purchases for sales promotions or premiums. Special editions, including personalized covers, corporate imprints, and excerpts, can be created in large quantities for special needs. For more information, contact the publisher.

We are always looking for people to write books on new and related subjects. If you have an idea for a book, please contact us at proposals@schifferbooks.com.

Chapter ~1~

If you're going to be trapped in a car for three hours—well, six hours round-trip—it's good to have a friend along, Oliver thought. And Sam was the closest thing he'd made to a friend yet, after almost six months in Maryland.

It was Ruby who suggested Oliver invite Sam. "Olls, you need to socialize," she had said the other day, in her most annoying older-sister tone. "What about inviting Sam along when we go to Monticello on Saturday?"

They had all been sitting around the dinner table. His parents, his two older sisters—Cassie, the nice one, and Ruby, the one he wished had stayed back in New Jersey when they moved—and himself. Everyone else immediately agreed, nodding and exclaiming about how, yes, Oliver did need to spend more time with kids his own age outside school, and yes, Sam was so great, and on and on.

Back in New Jersey, Oliver had spent lots of time with kids his own age. His best friends, Jared and Arlo, who were identical twins, lived right next door, and the three of them had been inseparable since they were babies.

Or so he'd been told. Things had been going fine. He had the twins to hang out with after school, and the twins—Ruby had named them "Jarlo" a long time ago, and the term had stuck—to sit with at lunch, and the twins to play with at recess.

And then, last year, his parents' company had offered his mom and dad new jobs in the Washington, DC, office, and they had to move in April, and all of a sudden everything changed.

"But what about the fifth-grade science fair project next year?" Oliver had said, stunned, when he first learned about the move. He and Jarlo had spent years planning for the fifth-grade science fair. They had a whole project in mind, involving cows and what happened to the gas they emitted. It was sure to win; he just knew it. And now Jared and Arlo—he texted and Facetimed with them a lot—were hard at work on the project. And Oliver was stuck in Bethesda, Maryland.

At his old school, everyone had known him since kindergarten, if not earlier. Now, he was still "the new kid," or "the noob," even if he had been there for almost half a year. He still didn't know anyone all that well. He didn't know what to say to them. And when he did open his mouth to say something, what came out wasn't always what he meant to say.

Like the other day in class. Ms. Martin, his fifth-grade teacher at Eastview Elementary, had been asking something about the Declaration of Independence, and Oliver, who had read a whole lot about the Declaration of Independence, meant to answer the question she had asked, but instead what he said was something about how Thomas Jefferson—who had written the Declaration of Independence—had slept in a bed that was set into a special alcove he had designed at his house.

Ms. Martin had looked puzzled but smiled kindly at Oliver. "Yes, Oliver, that's true," she said.

And then Oliver had launched into a series of facts he had memorized about the Declaration of Independence, including that fifty-six people had signed it. All men, no women, because women didn't have much power back then. That eight of the fifty-six were born in Britain. That Benjamin Franklin was the oldest signer.

As Oliver had rambled on, Tom, one of the popular kids, started laughing and then whispered something to Ryan, his best friend, and then the two of them were practically rolling on the floor.

"Brainiac," Tom gasped, between bouts of laughter. "Jeez, Oliver, does your brain ever stop?"

Well, no, it didn't. But Oliver somehow realized that wasn't the right answer. He stopped talking.

"Tom?" Ms. Martin said warningly. "Enough. And thanks, Oliver; that was very informative." She called on Ava, who was waving her hand in the air.

"Oliver had a good point about the women," Ava said. "Did you know that Abigail Adams wrote to John about that? She said, 'Remember the ladies.' But I guess that didn't accomplish much."

Lately Ava had been talking a lot about Abigail Adams and her husband, John Adams, the second president of the United States. Everyone in the class had done a project a couple of weeks earlier about a major figure in colonial America, and Ava had done hers on Abigail.

Oliver's had been on Thomas Jefferson, which was useful, since Oliver's family members—plus Sam—were currently in the car heading to Thomas Jefferson's house, Monticello. And Cassie and their mom were going to visit the University of Virginia, which was nearby. Cassie was a senior in high school. The thought of her going away to college next year was very stressful. It would be just him and Ruby, who was in ninth grade, at home with their parents.

Oliver glanced around the car. He and Sam were in the way back. Cassie and Ruby were in the middle, and his parents were in the front, busy discussing something that had happened at work. Cassie had her headphones on and was texting something on her phone. Ruby had her headphones on, too, and was reading a book.

"Oliver," Sam suddenly said. He hadn't said much so far. Sam often seemed to be off in his own world. But then, Oliver had been told that was the case with himself as well. So he probably should understand such behavior. "Did you finish the science project yet?"

Ms. Martin had asked everyone to write three paragraphs, accompanied by illustrations, about the experiment they had been doing in class, involving growing plants in water and observing them. Hydroponics.

Oliver nodded. It had been easy. "What about you?" He looked at Sam, who was wearing the hat he'd bought at the Mount Vernon gift shop a few weeks earlier on the fifth-grade field trip. It was one of those black tricornered hats that men in colonial America wore. But the amazing thing about the hat was that it talked! It took Sam—and on one memorable occasion, Oliver—back in time! They had met George Washington! Unfortunately, according to Sam, the hat was now very tired. It had been resting. And Sam wasn't sure it would ever do anything magical again.

It definitely seemed tired now. It was slumping on Sam's head. "My parents made me finish all my homework last night," Sam said. "So I could come with you today and not have to worry about it, and then have some free time tomorrow."

Sam, Oliver knew, used to have a best friend, Andrew. But Andrew now spent most of his time with Tom and Ryan, and Sam seemed unhappy. Which was why Ruby had seized upon the idea of Sam as a friend for Oliver.

Ruby really wanted to be a reporter when she grew up. She was working on the high school newspaper and had quickly attached herself to Mrs. Gupta, who lived down the street. Mrs. Gupta was the editor of the *Clarion*, a neighborhood newsletter that came out a few times a year, and she was apparently delighted to have an assistant. So Ruby was the first to know about anything going on. Including who was friends with whom.

"What's up with the hat?" Oliver asked, gesturing at Sam's head.

Sam sighed. "It's still asleep," he said. "I was kind of

hoping that since we're going to Thomas Jefferson's house, it would get all excited and wake up, but so far it hasn't." He sighed again.

Ruby had taken her headphones off, and she turned around to face Oliver and Sam. "What about the hat?" she said.

Oh no! The last thing Oliver needed was Ruby finding out about the hat's special qualities. She probably would put something in the high school newspaper about it, and in the *Clarion*, and Sam would get mad at him and not want to even sort of be his friend. The hat's magic abilities were to be kept secret, Oliver knew.

"Nothing," Oliver and Sam both said at the same time.

"You said something about it waking up," Ruby persisted.

"Um, like, sometimes I pretend it's a person," Sam said. "You know, like a funny joke." And he squirmed around in his seat. "Ha, ha," he said unconvincingly.

"Yeah," Oliver said, trying to be helpful. Sam usually was a good actor, but this time his skills seemed to have deserted him. Maybe he was nervous. "It's pretty funny." And Oliver mustered up a laugh.

"Uh-huh," Ruby said, a skeptical look in her eye. Oliver knew perfectly well that Ruby would come back to the topic of the hat at some later point. But for now, they had fended her off. "So, Sam," Ruby continued, fixing her gaze upon him. "Did you know there's a new family that just moved in next door to the park?"

Ruby had told Oliver about this family already. Apparently they had a son who, like Ruby, was a freshman in high school, and twins who were in fifth grade, a girl and a boy. Ruby was hoping to meet them and interview them for the newsletter. Oliver was kind of happy to hear about this new family. What if the kids, or even one of them, were in Ms. Martin's class? Then he wouldn't be the new kid anymore. That would be cool. He started imagining what would happen. Tom and Ryan would focus on these kids instead of on him. They could be the object of fascination. Oliver could fade into the background.

"Sam?" Ruby was asking. "Sam! God, you're just as bad as Oliver! You both need to pay attention when someone's talking to you!"

"Oh, sorry," Sam said, blinking.

Oliver just glared at her.

"You know my theory about our family?" Ruby said to Sam. No, not that again. Oliver groaned silently. He had heard this theory many times already. "So, Cassie got most of the social skills. She has tons of friends here already, you know? And she probably will get the lead in the school play, just like she always did in New Jersey. And there's this guy who really likes her."

Oliver looked over at Cassie, but she seemed oblivious, with her headphones on and her thumbs busily texting. Probably with some of those new friends.

"So there weren't a whole lot of social skills left over for me and poor Olls," Ruby continued. "I mean, I have some social skills—you have to have some to be a reporter, I think—but not as many as Cassie does. So I took what was left over. And poor Olls, well . . ." And Ruby paused and gave Oliver a pitying look.

"Can you just shut up?" Oliver said. She was so incredibly annoying. He must have some social skills, right? Or maybe she was correct. Maybe he didn't have any. Maybe that's why Tom still made fun of him and he still was "the noob" after almost six months. Maybe that's why he always said things that made people call him "brainiac." Which he didn't think was a compliment. Although being smart was a good thing, of course.

"Olls, close your mouth," Ruby said. "Don't breathe through your mouth all the time. It makes you look weird."

"Stop it!" Oliver said. "Just stop it! Stop it!"

Sam, fortunately, was staring out the window and didn't seem to be paying much attention. He was lucky. He was an only child.

"Could you both please stop arguing?" Cassie said, taking off her headphones and looking back and forth between Ruby and Oliver. "I can't hear my music."

"What's going on back there?" Oliver's mom said, also turning around. "Please, kids, can you try to get along a little better? We still have another hour or so until we get to Monticello."

"I was just pointing out . . ." Ruby began.

"Cut it out," Oliver's dad, who was driving, added. "Ruby and Ollie, you're going to have to be together all day, so this arguing isn't going to continue. I don't want to have to say anything more."

Oliver hated being called Ollie. Or Olls, for that matter. He tried to stop focusing on his family and focus instead on Thomas Jefferson. The third president of the United States. The author of the Declaration of Independence. The founder of the University of Virginia. Monticello had been a longtime project of Jefferson's. Situated on top of a mountain, it had been built over a period of many years. It was supposed to be very beautiful.

And then there was the part of Thomas Jefferson that Oliver found very confusing. He had written a document that stated that people were entitled to life, liberty, and the pursuit of happiness. And yet Thomas Jefferson had owned other people. He was a slave owner. He had had one family with his wife, and another family with an enslaved woman named Sally Hemings, so his own kids had been his slaves. How could he write the Declaration of Independence and yet own other people, including people who were related to him?

Oliver had asked Ms. Martin about this, and Ms. Martin had said it was an excellent question, and the class started discussing how someone could hold such opposite beliefs, and what they would ask Thomas Jefferson about slavery if they met him. He knew he'd have a lot of questions if he ever met Thomas Jefferson, that was for sure. He wondered if maybe the hat might wake up, and if maybe he and Sam—but not Ruby—could actually meet Thomas Jefferson. Go back in time to when he lived at Monticello. Back to the eighteenth and nineteenth centuries. Maybe . . .

"Here," Cassie was saying, interrupting Oliver's thoughts. "Why don't you and Sam play something on the iPad." She extended her iPad back toward Oliver.

"Oh, thanks," Oliver said. That's why Cassie was his preferred sister. By far. She actually cared about him. Unlike a certain other sister he could name.

Soon, he and Sam were involved with the iPad, and

before he knew it, the car had stopped. They were on a street. He had no idea where they were.

"Is this Monticello?" he asked. It couldn't be. It looked too ordinary.

"Jeez, Olls," Ruby said impatiently. "We're dropping Mom and Cassie off so they can see UVA. Remember?"

Oh, right. And then he and his dad and Sam and, unfortunately, Ruby, would go see Monticello and then pick his mom and Cassie up later. "Why don't you go with them," Oliver muttered, causing Ruby to scowl at him.

"Please behave," his mom said, getting out of the car after giving him and Ruby sharp looks.

"Have fun," Cassie said breezily, waving at them all. "Sorry to miss the squabbling."

"Can I sit up front now?" Ruby inquired, as their mom and Cassie headed down the street.

"Why not," their dad said wearily. "Just please don't argue with Ollie any more, okay?"

And before long, his dad pulled the car into a parking space in an outdoor lot, and the four of them made their way to a set of buildings, which included a gift shop, a café, and a museum with information about Thomas Jefferson. The actual house, Monticello, was atop the nearby hill.

As they settled into their seats on the shuttle bus that was taking them up the hill—Ruby and their dad were in front of Oliver and Sam—Oliver heard a voice. A familiar, high-pitched voice. One he hadn't heard for a couple of weeks.

"And where might we be?" the voice said.

"Oh, wow!" Sam exclaimed. A huge smile spread across his face. "I thought you might never wake up!"

The hat, for it was indeed the hat that was speaking, twisted itself around. "Never wake up! Sam! Have you no faith in me?" It bounced up and down on Sam's head, seeming very excited. "Be this Mr. Jefferson's house?"

"Yes!" Oliver said, also very excited. "It is."

The bus was winding its way up the mountain, and it stopped near the house, which was red brick, with white pillars and many windows with dark shutters.

"Construction began in 1769," the hat said in its squeaky voice. "And work was still going on into the 1800s. Mr. Jefferson had many plans for Monticello." Maybe the hat could get a job as a tour guide, Oliver thought. It seemed very well informed.

Oliver's dad and Ruby were standing up in preparation to get off the bus, and suddenly Oliver froze. Ruby was bound to hear the hat talking. He exchanged glances with Sam, who now was frowning. Maybe he was worrying about the same thing.

The hat, though, seemed to have no cares in the

world. Oliver supposed that after a couple-of-weeks-long nap, it was completely rejuvenated and filled with energy. It continued talking loudly.

"Did you know that the house has thirteen skylights?" the hat asked. "Did you know that it has forty-three rooms?" Actually, Oliver did know that. He had been studying the Monticello website in preparation for the trip. But how did the hat know it? "Well?" the hat said impatiently. "Sam and Oliver? Don't you answer when you're spoken to?" It sounded like Ruby, Oliver thought.

"Who said that?" Ruby asked, looking at Oliver and Sam.

They looked at each other. "He did," each of them blurted out, pointing at the other.

"That didn't sound like either one of you," Ruby said suspiciously.

"That's because it wasn't!" the hat said triumphantly. "It was I. And who might you be, young lady?"

"Very funny," Ruby said. "I guess you're a ventriloquist now, Sam?"

"Exactly," Sam said, looking relieved. "I've been studying ventriloquism. Yes."

"Ventriloquism." The hat sniffed. "Really, Sam."

Ruby smiled. "Wow, you're not bad," she said.

Oliver glanced over at his dad, who was preoccupied with a map of Monticello. The four of them were now standing in line to enter the house.

"Oh, thanks," Sam said modestly.

"There's a house tour, and also a tour that focuses on slavery," Oliver's dad said, lifting his head from the map. "I think we should start with the house tour, and then we can go on the tour about slavery. It's important to learn about everyone who lived here, not just Thomas Jefferson." And he returned his attention to the map.

"Your father is correct," the hat said. "Did you know that during his lifetime, Mr. Jefferson owned about 600 people?"

Oliver had known that too. It was so hard to understand.

"I didn't know that," Sam said, shaking his head, causing the hat to wobble slightly.

"You must have known that, if you said it," Ruby said accusingly.

"But he didn't say it—I did!" the hat replied.

"Oh, stop it, Sam," Ruby said, sounding annoyed. "You guys are just trying to mess with me, aren't you?"

"It was I, young lady," the hat retorted. "Sam is a good actor, but he is no ventriloquist. As Mr. Jefferson would say, 'Honesty is the first chapter in the book of wisdom.'" And it sniffed disapprovingly.

The tour group ahead of them moved into the house, leaving Oliver's group next in line. As they waited outside the front portico of Monticello, a guide started telling them things they should and shouldn't do while on the tour. Oliver found it difficult to focus on the instructions, given his worry that Ruby would figure out the hat's secret powers.

"Well, maybe I could be a ventriloquist, if I tried," Sam was saying indignantly to the hat.

Oliver recalled that the first time he had seen the hat in action, he, too, had thought it was Sam who was talking. But of course he had been quite wrong. Not that he was about to point that out to Ruby.

He glanced around. It really was beautiful around here, up on the mountain. He could see the countryside stretching out beneath them. The leaves on the neighboring hillsides and in the valleys were starting to turn shades of yellow and orange, it being mid-October.

"Oh, please," Ruby said, picking up the discussion. "You're both being so juvenile. Sam is talking, and that's all there is to it."

"No, he isn't!" the hat said, starting to jump up and down on Sam's head again. "I'm talking! I'm talking! I'm talking!"

Oh, no. This definitely wasn't good. Oliver glanced over at his dad, who was on the phone. Probably with his mom. "Oh, great!" he was saying. "So she's going to meet with those kids she knew from last year? See where they live?"

"I'll show you!" the hat said, and suddenly Oliver felt a dizzy feeling sweep over him. Sort of like what had happened when he and Sam went back in time to the crossing of the Delaware. When he had met George Washington. Was it about to happen again? He closed his eyes. He might as well just go with it, whatever was happening. He could hear screaming. It sounded like Ruby.

He opened his eyes, to find himself on a mountaintop. There was no sign of Monticello. Or of the lines of people waiting to take the tour. But there was Sam, and there was Ruby.

"Help!" she was screaming. Her eyes were practically bulging out of her head. "What the . . . Help! Olls, what the . . . Where are we? What's going on? Where's Dad? Where's Monticello? Oh my God!"

Oliver couldn't help grinning. This was kind of fun. Sam, though, who had the hat firmly perched on his head, was looking worried.

"I'm not sure it's such a great idea for your sister to know about the hat," he whispered to Oliver. "She won't keep it quiet."

Oliver nodded. He was concerned about that too. But it was almost worth it to see Ruby so upset.

And then a couple of teenage boys rode up on their horses. They were wearing strange clothes—pants that ended at the knees, with socks; vests over long-sleeved shirts with weird ruffled collars. One boy had reddish hair, which was pulled back in a ponytail of sorts. As their horses slowed, they stared at Oliver, Sam, and Ruby, who was trying to calm herself down.

"Okay," Ruby was saying to herself. "Okay. There's some explanation for this. I know there has to be." She took a series of deep breaths.

"Dabney, perhaps they are lost," the red-haired boy said, bringing his horse to a stop. "They have no horses."

"Are you well?" the other boy asked, also stopping, and looking at Ruby with concern. "I do hope you haven't taken sick or perhaps been startled at the sight of us." And he smiled at Ruby.

Ruby glared at Oliver, before tossing her hair around and smiling at both of the teenage boys. Oliver supposed she must be practicing her social skills on them. "Oh, no, I'm fine," she said. "But it's kind of you to ask."

Oliver and Sam exchanged glances. Could the red-headed boy possibly be Thomas Jefferson as a teenager? And who was Dabney? Oliver thought back. He remembered that as a teenager, Thomas Jefferson had a good friend who had ended up marrying one of Thomas Jefferson's sisters. Perhaps that was Dabney?

"We seem to have forgotten our manners," Dabney said. "I'm Dabney Carr, and my somewhat shy friend is Thomas Jefferson."

"Thomas Jefferson," Ruby said. She stared at the two of them, and then back at Oliver and Sam. And at the hat. Oliver could see that she was starting to put everything together. Her eyes narrowed. "Thomas Jefferson," she said again. "Well, okay, then. And Dabney Carr. Nice to meet you both. I'm Ruby, and this is my brother, Oliver, and his friend, Sam."

"A pleasure," Thomas Jefferson said.

"Isn't this a beautiful spot?" Dabney Carr said, gesturing expansively around him. "This wonderful mountain? Tom and I have decided that when one of us dies, one hopes a long time from now, the other one will bury him here."

"At Monticello?" Ruby asked. "Here?"

"Monticello," Thomas Jefferson said, a faraway look in his eye. "What a perfect name. Little mountain."

Ruby tossed her hair again. "Yes, quite perfect," she said. She smiled at both of the other teenagers. Ugh, Oliver thought. She was such a phony. She never smiled at Oliver. Except when she had gotten the better of him in one of their arguments.

Both Thomas Jefferson and Dabney Carr smiled back at her.

This was getting kind of annoying, Oliver thought. Like they were at an eighteenth-century version of a high school dance or something. Why did the hat have to bring Ruby along, anyway?

"Do you speak Italian?" she asked the older boys.

Yes, they did, Oliver knew. Or at least, he knew Thomas Jefferson did. Thomas Jefferson had gone to a one-room school as a teenager where he learned a whole variety of languages, including Latin, Greek, and Italian. He was very well educated. Oliver wouldn't mind learning a language himself. Next year in middle school, he was planning to study Chinese. He had heard it was very difficult, which was why he wanted to study it. It would be a good challenge. He had been encouraging Jarlo to study Chinese too. They could speak it to one another on their Facetime calls.

As Thomas Jefferson and Dabney Carr began explaining their school situation to Ruby, Oliver suddenly realized that his dad probably had no idea what was going on, and would undoubtedly be really upset. Maybe he'd be summoning the police to search for them. Maybe all of Monticello would be turned upside down in an effort to find them.

He expressed his concern to Sam, who shook his head.

"Parents never notice anything when this kind of thing happens," Sam said reassuringly. "At least, mine never do."

"High school, yes," Ruby was saying. "It's a much-larger school than yours. And I write for the newspaper." She started going on about how much she loved to write.

"As do I," Thomas Jefferson said. And they exchanged meaningful glances.

Jeez, Oliver thought. Would Thomas Jefferson fall in love with Ruby and they'd disrupt the whole pattern of history? Or maybe Dabney Carr would fall in love with Ruby and not end up marrying Thomas Jefferson's sister. But that couldn't happen, could it? And why would anyone fall in love with Ruby, anyway?

"Maybe we should be heading back," Sam said to Oliver. "This is all getting a little too high-schoolish." And he nodded toward the three teenagers. "They're not paying any attention to us at all. It wasn't like this with George. He always seemed interested in talking to me."

"Yeah," Oliver said. "I mean, I'd like to ask Thomas Jefferson a whole bunch of questions, but he seems to want to talk only to Ruby."

"Okay," Sam said. "I just need to take the hat off, and we'll be back." And he lifted the hat off his head. And then a second later the three of them were back at the front door of Monticello. Their group was being escorted in.

Chapter
~2~

Oliver felt somewhat breathless and stumbled slightly as they stepped into Monticello's front entrance hall. Its ceiling rose two stories high, and a balcony wrapped around the second floor. Some maps and paintings hung on the walls, and he could see a fireplace on one side.

He looked at Ruby, who was speechless for once. She seemed to be in something of a daze.

"Kids?" his dad said. "You all seem really out of it. What's going on?"

"Nothing," Ruby snapped. She cast a fierce eye upon Oliver and Sam.

Well, at least she wasn't saying anything to their dad about meeting the young Thomas Jefferson and his friend. Maybe that meant she wasn't going to tell anyone about it? He wasn't sure.

His dad shrugged. "Ollie? Sam?" he said. "You okay?"

They both nodded, and they all continued with the group into a series of rooms, which included Thomas Jefferson's study and his bedroom. Oliver was fascinated with some of Thomas Jefferson's inventions: a five-sided revolving stand so he could switch from one document to another when he was reading, a special elaborate clock, and of course his bed, which was indeed built into an alcove. One side of the bed opened up to his bedroom, and the other side to his study. He wondered if he, Oliver, could somehow go back to the eighteenth century again and tell Thomas Jefferson about the farting-cow science project. He probably would find it quite intriguing.

"Note the bust of Mr. Adams," the hat suddenly said, stirring on Sam's head.

Oliver looked over, and sure enough, there was a statue of John Adams. Thomas Jefferson's friend, and then enemy, and then friend again. Oddly enough, they died on the same day—July 4, 1826, fifty years after Independence Day 1776.

"Shhh," Sam said, glancing around nervously.

Oliver looked around too. His father was engaged in conversation with one of the guides, and Ruby still seemed completely out of it. She was staring glassily around Thomas Jefferson's study.

"Don't shush me, Sam," the hat said, sounding peevish. "I have much information to impart! Mr. Jefferson and Mr. Adams had quite a complicated relationship. But it all turned out well in the end."

Sam grabbed onto Oliver's

John Adams Bust, at Monticello

arm and pulled him into the next room—Thomas Jefferson's bedroom—away from Oliver's dad and Ruby.

"What should we do?" Sam said, sounding slightly panicked. "About your sister? About the hat and all? What if she tells everyone? This is kind of a private thing. I mean, just Nigel and J.P. and you knew about it."

Nigel was Sam's cousin, who was in college and lived with Sam's family. J.P. was Ava's stepbrother, who was in third grade.

"And all of you managed to keep it quiet," Sam continued. "Which was kind of surprising in the case of J.P. But the way your sister's so into being a reporter, I'm stressing out. What if she reports on it? I mean, my mom's a reporter too, but parents don't seem to pick up on any of this, so that wasn't a problem. But . . ."

"Sam, really," the hat said. Somehow it seemed to be shaking its head. "Surely you must know that what needs to be known will be known, all in its own good time, and what doesn't will be kept quiet. As Mr. Jefferson would say, 'How much pain have cost us the evils which have never happened.'" And it stopped talking.

Oliver wasn't exactly sure what the hat meant, but he thought maybe what it was trying to say was that they shouldn't worry. That Ruby wouldn't end up saying anything. That it would be all right. He asked Sam if he agreed, and Sam nodded.

"I think that's what it meant too." Sam said. "But we need to talk to her. Like, soon."

But they didn't have an opportunity until they had finished touring the inside of the house and were outside, waiting for the start of the tour about the enslaved people at Monticello. Oliver's dad had wandered off down a pathway, and the three of them were standing outside the back of the building, near a garden.

Oliver glanced at Ruby. She seemed less dazed. More like herself.

"What happened back there?" she asked, looking back and forth between Oliver, Sam, and the hat. "This has to do with your hat, doesn't it, Sam? And you guys knew about this before, right? That this might happen?"

"Um, well," Sam began.

"Of course it has to do with me," the hat said loudly, sounding proud of itself. "I am the one who organizes all of this travel."

"And this isn't you talking, Sam, is it?" Ruby said, frowning at Sam. "You really don't know anything at all about ventriloquism, do you?"

"Um, well," Sam said again, shifting nervously around. "I mean, I'd like to learn about ventriloquism. In fact, I might take a class in ventriloquism. Maybe this winter."

"That really was Thomas Jefferson, wasn't it?" Ruby said. "And his friend. And the hat took us there, and then it took us back here. This is just so amazing. I mean, how did it happen exactly?"

"Look," Oliver said desperately. "You're not going to write about this, are you? This is Sam's hat. It's his thing. He doesn't want you to report on it. Please?" He knew he sounded wimpy, but he couldn't help it. Ruby could be merciless. Sometimes the only way to handle her was to act powerless. And then she'd take pity on him.

"Report on it?" Ruby scoffed. "Like, no way! I mean, who'd believe me? They'd think I was completely insane. I'd never get another assignment again! Jeez, Olls, I mean, really!"

Oliver could see Sam heaving a sigh of relief. He felt lighter and happier himself. The hat had been right. There had been nothing to worry about with Ruby. At least, not when it came to that particular issue.

A woman bustled up to them. "Are you here for the tour?" she inquired. She was wearing a name tag, so Oliver assumed she must be the tour guide.

"We're very interested in finding out how Thomas Jefferson could write the Declaration of Independence and yet own slaves," Oliver began. He hadn't had a chance to ask Thomas Jefferson himself, but perhaps this guide could provide some assistance.

Other people started to gather around, including Oliver's dad. The tour guide smiled at Oliver and nodded. "Yes, that's the big question, isn't it? Let's wait till we're sure everyone's here, and we'll get to that."

She checked her watch and waited for a few more people to arrive before she began. She started by describing the cabins that lined the pathway they were standing on, known as Mulberry Row. Enslaved people had lived in them, often many members of a family per cabin.

As Oliver and the others clustered into a cabin to take a look, he had a sudden impulse to ask Sam if he could borrow the hat. Just for a minute.

"Okay," Sam said. "But be really careful with it."

As soon as Oliver put the hat on, he felt that dizzy sensation again, and suddenly he was face to face with a boy about his age. Oliver looked around, through the dim light in the cabin. There was no one else in the room. Sam and the others were nowhere to be seen. But he could hear voices outside, calling to one another.

"Who are you?" the boy asked, looking a little frightened. "You were not there, and then all of a sudden . . ."

Was he back in the eighteenth century again? Did this boy live in the cabin? What exactly was going on here? He felt somewhat bewildered.

"Oliver," Oliver managed to say. "I'm Oliver. What year is it?"

The boy gave him a strange glance. "Why, it is the year 1815," he said. "How do you not know the year? Are you a traveler from afar?"

Oliver peered more closely at the boy. He was wearing worn-looking pants and a much-mended cotton shirt. He had a pale complexion and a quizzical look on his face. So this was the nineteenth century. Thomas Jefferson must be old by now.

"Yes," Oliver managed to say. "From Maryland. But before that, New Jersey."

"Oh, up north," the boy said. "I would like to go there one day." And his expression turned wistful. "Madison Hemings," he said, nodding at Oliver. "I live here. But a long time ago, my mother lived in Paris. France, you know. Across the sea."

Madison Hemings! This was Sally Hemings's son. And therefore Thomas Jefferson's son. And therefore an enslaved person. Oliver tried frantically to remember more details about Madison Hemings. There was a lot he'd like to discuss with him.

"I like your hat," Madison Hemings said, gesturing at it. "I have not seen one quite like that before."

"Thanks," Oliver said. "Here, you want to take a look?" He took off the hat, and then all of a sudden Madison Hemings wasn't there any more. In fact, no one was there at all. "Shoot," he said, remembering what Sam had told him about the hat—that it had to remain on one's head at all times or one would end up back in the twenty-first century with no warning. Which must be what had just happened. He really wanted to find Madison Hemings again.

"No," the hat said squeakily, seeming to guess what Oliver was thinking. "I must remain upon your head. Perhaps you will have another chance at some point to speak with young Mr. Hemings, Oliver, but for the moment, we should go back outside and find the others."

Oliver reluctantly agreed. The group had moved down the pathway toward another building, and the guide was discussing the type of work the enslaved population did at Monticello. He caught up to Sam, who gave him a curious look.

". . . making nails," the tour guide was saying. She pointed at Sam and Oliver. "About the age of you two. Take the year 1796," she continued. "Did you know that of the fourteen nailers that year, eight of them were between the ages of ten and twelve?" Oliver and Sam looked at each other, horrified. "That's right. And they most likely worked from sunrise to sunset, every day except Sunday. So in winter, their work day was, say, nine hours, but in summer, it could be fourteen hours long."

Oliver tried to picture himself and Sam spending fourteen hours a day making nails. He wasn't even sure how to make nails.

He raised his hand. "How do you make nails, anyway?"

The guide launched into a description of how the nail rods were brought from Philadelphia and then hammered into nails, and that eventually Thomas Jefferson got a machine that cut the nails. She glanced down at a piece of paper. "Mr. Jefferson wrote in his farm book, 'Children till 10 years old to serve as nurses. From 10 to 16 the boys make nails, the girls spin. At 16 go into the ground or learn trades.'"

Kids younger than ten were nurses? And what did "go into the ground" mean?

But the guide was moving them along, and other people were asking questions, and soon the tour was over. And he hadn't even gotten a chance to ask her more about Thomas Jefferson owning slaves.

"That was really fascinating," Ruby was saying. "I'm glad I got to ask her more about how Thomas Jefferson could have owned slaves and written the Declaration of Independence."

She had? When? Could it have been when he was talking with Madison Hemings in the cabin? And he had missed it. But he didn't want to tell her anything about that. He supposed talking with Madison Hemings was more fascinating than talking with the tour guide, anyway.

"You should go back in time and talk to him, Ruby," their dad said. "To Thomas Jefferson. Pin him down like a good reporter on all of his contradictions." And he smiled fondly at her.

Ruby smiled back, but she looked a little troubled. Maybe she had spent too much time practicing her social skills on Thomas Jefferson instead of asking the tough questions, Oliver thought.

"What happened back there?" Sam hissed at Oliver, as Ruby and Oliver's dad headed back down the pathway. "When you borrowed the hat?"

"I met Madison Hemings!" Oliver said, feeling somewhat guilty that Sam hadn't gotten to come along. "He told me about how his mom lived in Paris."

"Did he say anything about his dad?" Sam asked.

Oliver shook his head. He found himself imagining all the people who had lived at Monticello—Thomas Jefferson, hanging out in his beautiful study, writing and reading and inventing, and boys Oliver's own age working from dawn to dusk making nails. The whole thing seemed completely wrong.

Soon, they were back in the car, heading toward the University of Virginia to pick up his mom and Cassie. His dad and Ruby were sitting up front, and he and Sam were in the middle seats. His dad put the radio on and Ruby put on her headphones.

"Mr. Jefferson taught himself architecture," the hat piped up from atop Sam's head. "Mr. Jefferson designed the University of Virginia as what he called an 'academical village.'" It paused and seemed to turn toward Oliver. "Perhaps your sister will attend classes there next year, although when it opened in 1825, there were of course no female students. They were first admitted only in 1970."

The hat rambled on some more about UVA, and Oliver's mind drifted on to other things. He wondered if he'd have another chance to go back and meet Thomas Jefferson or Madison Hemings. He wondered if the new family who had moved in near the park would be nice. He wondered what Jarlo were doing right now. He really missed Jarlo. He sighed.

Ruby had pulled her headphones off. "We're here!" she exclaimed, as their dad pulled the car into a parking garage. "Can we get out and walk around the campus too? I mean, maybe I'd like to go here one day."

The sooner the better, Oliver thought, but he didn't say anything.

"Sure," his dad said. "Maybe Oliver or Sam would like to go here one day too." He smiled at all of them. "We're meeting them at the big statue of Thomas Jefferson."

Ruby started talking about events that had happened in Charlottesville in recent years, and asking their dad about race relations today compared with how things were in Thomas

Jefferson
Statue at UVa

Jefferson's time, and Oliver wanted to listen but then his dad's phone rang.

"Oh, sure, Jared," his dad said "And Arlo. He's right here." And he handed the phone to Oliver.

Oliver could see Sam looking at him curiously again. Had he ever mentioned Jarlo to Sam? He wasn't sure. Maybe Sam thought Oliver had never had any friends, ever. Just because he didn't really have any in Maryland.

"Hey, dudes," Oliver said, torn between feeling delighted to talk to Jarlo and annoyed that he still didn't have his own phone. "I was just thinking of you guys." Of course, Jarlo didn't have their own phones, and Sam didn't seem to have one either. Neither did Ava, he knew, but some of the kids in his class already did. He was envious.

"So, the science project," Jarlo said in unison. They often talked that way, Oliver reflected. "We want to get your input," Jared said. He usually took over the conversation. Arlo was quieter. "Did you see that article about how the cow gas is even more of a problem than they already thought? And it's methane gas that they're farting, right? So this ties even more into the whole climate change thing. And . . ."

Oliver hadn't seen the article. He listened as Jared continued to describe the science project, and how Mr. Porter, the fifth grade teacher who was supposed to be the coolest teacher at his old school, really liked the idea, and how they were working with this kid Arun who was super-smart, and . . .

"Wait," Oliver said. "Arun is taking over my part in the project?" He felt a pang shoot through him.

There was a pause on the line. Oliver noticed that

his dad, Ruby, and Sam were way ahead of him. His dad turned around and gestured for him to catch up. The three of them were waiting near a gigantic bronze statue of Thomas Jefferson that stood in front of a large red-brick building with white columns and a dome. Sort of Monticello-esque but much bigger. Thomas Jefferson definitely seemed to favor a certain architectural style, Oliver thought. But then he turned his mind back to Jarlo. This wasn't good. The idea had always been that Jarlo would do the project. With long-distance help from Oliver. Not Jarlo and Arun. Just Jarlo.

"Well, like, you're not here anymore," Jared finally said.

"Yeah, and we needed a third person in the group," Arlo chimed in. "And Arun is really into farting cows, just like we are. But we'll still check in with you, okay?"

Oliver's stomach was starting to hurt. He wasn't sure what to say. It was one thing not to know what to say with the kids in Maryland, but not to know what to say with Jarlo? This had never happened before.

"Oliver?" Arlo was saying. "Are you still there?"

"I think we lost the connection," Jared said. "Oliver?"

Oliver pushed the button on the phone and disconnected the call. Let them think whatever they wanted. He felt as if . . . as if . . . well, as if he might start to cry. But he couldn't let that happen. Couldn't let Sam see him crying. Or Ruby. Especially Ruby.

"Olls, don't dawdle like that," Ruby was saying as he approached the three of them and the giant statue. "You're keeping everyone waiting."

"You're not my mom," Oliver snapped at her. Actually,

his mom didn't always tell him what he was doing wrong all the time. Just Ruby did. He handed the phone back to his dad.

"Ollie?" his dad asked. "Everything okay?"

"Yeah," he said. He didn't really want to say anything more. He looked up at the statue. Thomas Jefferson was looking slightly off to the left, holding some kind of document or other. He was wearing a long jacket or coat and knee-length pants. He looked a lot older than the teenager Oliver and the others had met.

Maybe the statue would start talking to him. Or maybe the hat could take them back again. But the hat wasn't saying anything.

"Hey, there's your mom," Sam suddenly said, pointing. "And Cassie."

Indeed, there they were. They were talking intently about something but started waving at the group as soon as they saw them.

"Wow," Cassie said as they approached. "So I went to see this girl's dorm room, who I sort of knew from last year, and it was totally amazing!" She started describing the room, and the campus tour she and their mom had taken, and their mom was adding various comments and asking questions about the Monticello tour, and Ruby and their dad were asking questions about UVA, and the six of them started walking around the campus, but Oliver couldn't concentrate on what he was seeing or hearing. Nothing was making sense. The science fair project was something he and Jarlo had thought about forever. Probably since first grade or something. And now they had replaced him! It was so unfair. Why did his family have to move, anyway?

The hat suddenly cleared its throat. "Peace and friendship with all mankind is our wisest policy, and I wish we may be permitted to pursue it," it said. "Something Mr. Jefferson once wrote."

"Can you explain yourself more clearly?" Sam asked it. The other four were up ahead, so only the two boys were in earshot of the hat. "You're always saying these things I can't really understand."

"Friendship, my dear Sam," the hat said, sounding a bit impatient. "I was speaking of friendship."

"Is this about me and Andrew again?" Sam said. "You know, I've actually shot some hoops with him once or twice lately, so maybe . . ."

"Actually, no," the hat said. "I was directing my remarks to Oliver. In fact, I think it might be wise for you to lend me to Oliver for a week or so," it continued thoughtfully.

Really? Oliver felt his spirits rise slightly.

"What?" Sam said. "But . . ."

"Lend. Borrow," the hat said.

"Nothing permanent. Oliver should borrow me for a week or so."

"Why?" Sam asked, sounding upset. "I mean, I thought you and I . . ."

"Sam, we have a bond," the hat said. "Most definitely. But, again to quote Mr. Jefferson, 'Our greatest happiness does not depend on the condition of life in which chance has placed us, but is always the result of a good conscience, good health, occupation, and freedom in all just pursuits.' Mr. Jefferson had a quote for almost any situation."

"Well, I'm not sure what you mean," Sam said. "But okay." And he took the hat off his head and handed it to Oliver.

"Really?" Oliver said. "Are you sure?"

Sam nodded. "If the hat says so, then okay."

The hat bounced up and down on Oliver's head, signaling its approval. And on the car ride back home, Oliver was able to forget about Jarlo and the science fair for a while, and he and Sam played some more games on the iPad, and it almost seemed like maybe things would be all right.

The next day was Sunday, and Ruby decided to drag Oliver over to the park, which was a couple of blocks away. She wanted to interview the new family for the *Clarion*, and they lived right next door to the park.

"Bring the basketball," she ordered. "If the Rodriguezes aren't home, at least we'll have something to do." Ruby was good at sports. In fact, she had been on a basketball team back in New Jersey and often scored most of the points. Oliver had been on a basketball team too. He wasn't the worst on the team—probably Arlo was—but he wasn't the best, either.

As they approached the park, Oliver could see some kids already there. The half of the park on one side of the street featured swings and climbing equipment. He could see Ava's stepbrother, J.P., swinging back and forth. Ava was standing next to him, leaning against the post that held the row of swings up. The two of them seemed to be arguing about something.

Ruby was heading for the other half of the park, which included a circular walking path and a basketball court. "See those kids over there?" she called to Oliver. "I think it might be them." And she continued in their direction.

"Hey, Oliver!" J.P. yelled over to him. "Why are you wearing Sam's hat?"

Oliver was startled. For a minute, he had forgotten he was wearing the hat. It hadn't said anything more once they had left UVA, and Sam had informed Oliver that it was unlikely to do much for a while. It was old. It was tired.

Oliver had nodded.

"Sam lent it to me," Oliver said now.

J.P. looked surprised. "Dude!" he exclaimed. "Can I have it for a while? I think Sam would be okay with that."

"No, he wouldn't," Ava snapped, much to Oliver's relief. "That's completely out of the question." Ava and J.P. exchanged a look, one that Oliver didn't understand.

"Yeah, okay," J.P. said, nodding. "Hey, you have a ball?" he asked, eyeing Oliver's basketball. "Let's go shoot some hoops over there. Come on!" And he jumped off the swing and ran off in the direction of the basketball court.

"God, he's such a pain," Ava said, shaking her head.

Oliver knew what she meant. Siblings could be so annoying. He glanced off toward the basketball court, where he could see Ruby. She was talking to three kids, one of whom looked taller than the other two.

"Do you think that's the new family?" Ava asked. "With the twins in our grade? I wonder if they'll be in Ms. Martin's class. Then you won't be the new kid anymore, right? How do you feel about that?"

Oliver knew that Ava's mom was some kind of therapist

or psychiatrist or something, and Ava had a tendency to ask people how they felt about things. Ava also wrote things all the time. Sort of like Ruby. Except Ava seemed to want to be a fiction writer, not a reporter. Her fictional characters must always be expressing their feelings, Oliver thought.

"Oh, well," Oliver said, not sure how to answer this. "Good, I guess. Being new isn't so great."

Ava nodded, as the two of them headed over to the basketball court. "It must be hard," she said thoughtfully. "Yeah. I mean, I've lived in the same house for as long as I can remember. But then I go to California every summer and most vacations, where my dad lives. So I can kind of relate."

Oliver considered this. Moving back and forth across the country must be hard too. He wondered what that would be like. You'd fly to California, and then you'd fly back to Maryland, and you'd keep doing that until you were grown up? You'd have different friends in each place and do different activities? You'd live in two houses in two neighborhoods?

"Hey," J.P. called. "Come on! The new kids want to play too!"

J.P. was talking to two dark-haired kids, a boy and a girl. "This is Colin, and this is Rhiannon," he announced. "They're in fifth grade and they're new!"

Oliver could see Ruby deep in conversation with the older boy. She was doing the same thing she had done with Thomas Jefferson and Dabney Carr. She was tossing her hair around and smiling at him. Except that she also had her phone out and seemed to be in the middle of interviewing him. She should have tried to interview Thomas Jefferson and Dabney Carr. Except that maybe cell phones and recording devices wouldn't work back then. Would they? They probably wouldn't, since they hadn't been invented yet? Although Thomas Jefferson would undoubtedly be fascinated by them. Ruby could always have used the old-fashioned method, of course. A pen and a notebook. That would have worked.

"Hey," Colin said, waving casually over at Oliver and Ava and interrupting Oliver's train of thought. "Pass me the ball?" And he gestured at Oliver. Oliver bounced it over to him, and Colin dribbled across to the hoop at the far side and gracefully, effortlessly, tossed the basketball in its direction. The ball swished through, barely moving the net.

"Dude!" J.P. said, his eyes wide. "Do that again!"

Colin laughed, retrieved the ball, bounced it a couple of times, and swished it through again.

"Show me how to do that," J.P. begged.

"Come on, R.," Colin said, gesturing toward his sister. "She's pretty good too." He tossed Rhiannon the ball, and the two of them started taking turns, making every single shot they took.

Oliver was transfixed. This was better than Ryan or Tom, who were the acknowledged best boys at sports in the whole fifth grade. Better than Katie, who was the best girl at sports in the whole fifth grade. Even Oliver knew that.

"Take a shot, dude," Colin said, waving at J.P. to come over.

As J.P. took a few shots, missing most of them, Ava turned toward Oliver. "This should be interesting tomorrow at school," she said. "Like, Ryan and Tom, you know? They're going to freak." She looked over toward Ruby and the older boy. "Is your sister interviewing him?" she inquired. "For the *Clarion*?"

"She's practicing her social skills," Oliver said. It was

kind of obvious what Ruby was doing, seeing as how the two of them, Ruby and Oliver, weren't up to Cassie's standards, and Ruby seemed to feel that was a problem.

Ava laughed. "That's a good one," she said.

Oliver wasn't sure why that was funny, but he laughed too, to be polite. "Yeah," he said uncertainly.

"You guys want to play?" Colin said to Ava and Oliver. "Come on."

He seemed perfectly friendly, not like Tom and Ryan, who always made him feel like they were doing him a big favor if they let him join in on whatever game the boys were all playing at recess. So Oliver nodded. Soon all five of them were on the basketball court, even though the twins were much better than the other three. Oliver even made a couple of baskets. And a few minutes later, Ruby came over with the older boy. Ruby was good, Oliver knew, but these kids were better. He wondered about the older brother.

"No, the twins got all the athletic ability in the family," he was saying to Ruby.

Kind of like the social skills in his family, Oliver thought. He wondered if Ruby would start talking about that, but miraculously she didn't.

Oliver had the ball, and he tossed it over to Ruby, who slipped her phone into her pocket and dribbled the ball over. She made a shot from halfway across the court, and Colin raised his eyebrows.

"Man," he said. "That was amazing!"

Rhiannon nodded. She hadn't said anything at all, Oliver noticed.

"Cool," the older boy said. "So, Ruby, do you want to

try to interview my parents now?"

"Sure," Ruby said, handing the ball over to Oliver, and she and the older boy headed toward their house.

So let's say Ruby has all the athletic skills, and Cassie has all the social skills—where did that leave him? Oliver wondered, as he took a shot and missed.

"Nice hat," Colin said, gesturing at Sam's hat on Oliver's head. "Where'd you get it?"

"Oh, I borrowed it from a friend," Oliver said. Was Sam his friend? Maybe. He wasn't sure.

"It's Sam's hat," J.P. chimed in. "He lives across the street from us. He's in fifth grade too. Like everyone here except me."

"It's an American colonial hat," Rhiannon suddenly said. "Popular in the time of the Revolutionary War. But you probably already knew that. But did you know that it allowed the wearers to show off their wigs more effectively than previous styles of hats?"

Wow, that was interesting. And it wasn't something Oliver already knew. He was impressed.

"R.'s like a walking encyclopedia," Colin said.

A walking encyclopedia? He had been described that way himself, Oliver reflected.

"Soldiers wore them, and they would put the point of the hat in front so they could see better from the sides," Rhiannon added.

"Cool," J.P. said. "When I saw George . . ."

Ava shot him a look, and he stopped. Oliver wondered what J.P. had been about to say. When he saw George who? He remembered Sam saying that J.P. knew about the hat. Could J.P. have gone back with Sam to see

George Washington? And what did Ava know? It was puzzling.

"So whose class are you in?" Ava said, clearly trying to change the subject. She turned toward Colin and Rhiannon.

"Ms. Martin," Colin said. "Both of us."

"That's great!" Ava said. "I love Ms. Martin. I'm in her class too. So's Oliver." She started talking about the wonders of Ms. Martin, and how she and her best friend Samantha were in Ms. Martin's after-school creative writing class, and how inspiring Ms. Martin was, and how lucky the twins were to be assigned to her.

Oliver agreed. He liked Ms. Martin a lot.

"Where did you live before?" Ava inquired.

"All over," Colin said. "England, Spain, other places."

"The longest we've ever lived anywhere is three years," Rhiannon added. "To be specific, two years and three hundred and twenty days. I was hoping we'd get to exactly three years, but it didn't work out that way. Our shortest was five hundred and thirty-three days. But we were really young then, so we don't remember it. Although Nico does. Our brother, that is."

"Eastview's a pretty cool place," J.P. said. "I think you guys will definitely enjoy it. I'd give it my stamp of approval. You know what, Ava? I'm really hungry. Can we go home now?"

Ava sighed. "Yeah, okay," she said. "Great to meet you guys, and see you tomorrow!" She and J.P. departed.

Just then, Ruby emerged with Nico from the new family's house. "Hey, Olls," she called over to Oliver. "I'm going to write this interview up now and email it to Mrs. Gupta."

Oliver figured he might as well go home with Ruby. Maybe he could talk the hat into waking up. He scooped up the basketball and started dribbling it down the pathway toward the street.

"Bye," Colin said. Rhiannon nodded.

"Bye," Oliver said, and he ran to catch up with Ruby.

"So they've lived all over the world," Ruby began. "England, Spain, New York. Their mom's English and their dad's Spanish, and they both work for international banks. But they've gone to American schools in all those other countries, which is why they sound American."

Oliver pondered this information. Maybe it was hard for him to move from New Jersey to Maryland, but these kids were moving all over the place. From one country to another. Only staying in one place for less than three years. Was it hard for them?

"Consider that, Olls," Ruby said. "Consider that for them, moving from New Jersey to here—just one move— must seem, like, totally easy."

Or maybe not, Oliver thought. Maybe it wasn't easy. Maybe moving was hard no matter how many times you had to do it.

They pushed open the front door. Oliver retreated up to his room, closed the door, and took off the hat.

"Are you ever going to wake up?" Oliver said, placing the hat into the Mount Vernon gift shop bag that Sam had given him.

"This is the hat's home," Sam had told him. "Sort of like its nest. It likes to sleep in here."

Now, the hat seemed to stir slightly. "Ah yes," it said. "Oliver. And I assume you would be interested in meeting

Mr. Jefferson again?"

Oliver nodded. Would the hat wake up enough to take him somewhere? Like, now?

"Do you know who Patrick Henry was?" the hat inquired.

"'Give me liberty or give me death,'" Oliver quoted. It was the only thing he could remember about Patrick Henry. Hadn't Patrick Henry said that at some point during the Revolutionary War period?

"Well, yes," the hat said, now sounding fully awake. "Patrick Henry did say that, in 1775. He was another Virginian, like Mr. Jefferson and General Washington. Another leader for the revolutionary cause against the British. But I actually wanted to explore something earlier on in the careers of Mr. Henry and Mr. Jefferson."

Oliver nodded. "Yeah, okay," he said. That sounded good. Whatever the hat suggested was fine with him.

"Very well," the hat said. "Please remove me from this bag at once!"

It really was a very bossy hat, Oliver reflected. But he did as he was asked.

"As a young man, Mr. Jefferson studied the law. And one of the friends he met was another young man named Patrick Henry, who was soon elected to the Virginia House of Burgesses. The legislature, you know," the hat said. "Of course, they were at odds later on."

Oliver nodded again.

"Well?" the hat said impatiently.

"Well?" Oliver asked in turn, not sure what the hat wanted him to do.

"Put me on your head!" the hat commanded. "Obviously!"

Just then, a knock sounded at his door.

"Oliver?" It was Cassie. Oh no! "Hey, Oliver, Mom says you have Tae Kwon Do now, and I need to walk you over to the studio."

Really? This was such bad timing. And why did his parents insist on having someone walk him to the studio? It was only about ten minutes away. If he had a phone, maybe they'd give him more independence because they'd know where he was. He'd tried that argument with them, but he hadn't succeeded.

"And what, pray tell, is Tae Kwon Do?" the hat asked, sounding confused.

Oliver sighed. "It's a martial art. From Korea."

"A martial art from Korea!" the hat exclaimed. "And you study this art? How extremely fascinating! Perhaps you will demonstrate?"

"Well . . ." Oliver began. Tae Kwon Do was another problem. Just like Jarlo and the science fair. This move to Maryland had messed absolutely everything up. He and Jarlo had started Tae Kwon Do lessons at a studio near their house in New Jersey when they were all still in preschool, and the three of them had been about to get their black belts at the end of fourth grade—and then Oliver had to move. The studio here seemed a lot stricter, and the new Tae Kwon Do master had told him he'd need more time before he could be tested for his black belt, and Jarlo had gotten their black belts over the summer, and Oliver sort of wanted to quit the whole thing because he felt so discouraged, but his parents had made him continue.

Cassie knocked again. "Hey, Ollie, what's going on?" she asked. "Come on! We have to go now!"

"Ah well," the hat said. "Later. I shall rest now." And it curled up and seemed to snore gently.

Oliver replaced the hat in the Mount Vernon bag and reluctantly opened the door.

"Get your Tae Kwon Do stuff ready!" Cassie was saying. "Who were you talking to in there?"

"Myself," Oliver said. He didn't want to say anything to Cassie about the hat. Miraculously enough, Ruby seemed to have kept her mouth shut about it.

"So what's going on with that hat?" Cassie said, as if reading Oliver's mind, as the two of them headed out the door to walk over to the Tae Kwon Do studio. "Why did Sam give it to you, anyway?"

"He just lent it to me," Oliver said. "For a week or so."

"Nice," Cassie said. She was walking along, talking to Oliver and texting at the same time.

If only he had a phone. But whom would he text, anyway? Jarlo seemed to be all friendly with Arun now, and maybe they wouldn't want to talk to him anymore. He sighed again.

"Are you okay, Ollie?" Cassie said, putting her phone into her pocket and focusing on him. "You've seemed really down lately."

"Um . . ." Oliver wasn't sure where to start. Jarlo. The science fair project. Arun. Tae Kwon Do. Tom and Ryan. Brainiac. Noob.

"Look, it's been hard for me too," Cassie said. "The move, I mean. I know you were really looking forward to fifth grade back home, just like I was looking forward to senior year with all my friends, so I totally get it."

Oliver was shocked. It was hard for Cassie? The one with the social skills? "But Ruby said . . ." he started.

Cassie waved one hand around in a dismissive kind of way. "I know Ruby means well, at least most of the time, but you can't always take everything she says so seriously," she said.

Ruby means well? He didn't think so. "She said you're the one with all the social skills, and there weren't many left over for her and me, and she took what was left over, and I'm just, like, hopeless."

Cassie looked at him and shook her head. "Oh, jeez, Ollie, that's awful," she said. "And it's not true either. I didn't take all the social skills. It's not so easy to come into a new school at the end of junior year, and I really miss all my old friends, and, yeah, there are some nice kids here, but most of the time that I'm texting? It's with my old friends, okay? And you have plenty of skills. You're totally amazing."

"And, like, Jarlo's working with Arun on the farting-cow project, and Jarlo already have their black belts now, and, I mean, Sam is okay, but he's not really my friend, and Ms. Martin is really great but sometimes in class I feel like what I'm saying just comes out wrong, and I never know what to say to all these new kids, and I wish we'd never moved."

Cassie reached over and patted him on the back. "Yeah, I feel like that a lot too," she said. "Not about farting-cow projects, but about the play they're doing this fall back home, and everyone thought I'd end up getting the lead role, and now I'm here and I'm not sure I'll even get into any plays at all. And then I'm really stressing out about college applications, and it's all just a lot to think about."

Somehow this was making him feel better. Not that he didn't feel bad for Cassie, but it was good to know he wasn't alone. "I'm stressed out about you going to college too," Oliver confessed. "You're leaving me here with Ruby."

Cassie laughed. "You crack me up," she said, as they approached the doorway to the studio. "So I'm going to go home now, and Mom's going to pick you up after class, okay? And just remember, you're the best brother ever."

"And you're the best sister," he said. Certainly better than Ruby. He waved goodbye to Cassie and headed up the stairway to the studio. A bunch of kids were already there, in their uniforms, for the red belt class. He was a red belt with five black stripes, the highest rank before black belt.

"Hey, Oliver." It was Katie, from Ms. Martin's class. She was a one-striper. "So I hear there are some new kids starting tomorrow? Twins?"

Oliver nodded, pleased to be in the know for once. "I met them today. A boy and a girl. They're really good at sports. Like you."

"Cool," Katie said.

Oliver went into the boys' locker room to change, and when he came out, the class was just starting.

"We'll be having exams next month," Master T was saying. He had a long name that no one could ever remember. "After class I'd like to speak with a few of you about getting ready for your black-belt exams." And he called off three names, including Oliver's.

Oliver couldn't believe it. A shock of excitement ran through him. This was really amazing. Would he at long last get to take the black-belt exam? As the hour-long class progressed, he found it difficult to focus on the combinations and one-steps they were reviewing. If he got to take the exam, that would be so incredible. He wanted to discuss the whole thing with the hat. Or with Thomas Jefferson. Or possibly Madison Hemings. He wondered if either of them had ever heard of Tae Kwon Do. Probably not.

"Oliver?" Master T said. "Are you paying attention?"

"Yes, sir," Oliver said, although it was fairly clear he hadn't been.

Finally the class was over, and Master T summoned the three of them in to his office. "I think you're all ready for your exam next month, but you have to keep practicing. Keep your focus. Come to as many classes as you can, all right?" And he continued on.

But Oliver was so happy he was barely listening. As soon as the meeting was over, he rushed out the door and down the stairs, where his mom was waiting.

"I get to take the black-belt exam next month!" he said.

"Oh, that's so great, honey," his mom said. "I know all of this has been hard for you, and I'm so proud of you." And she gave him a hug.

Oliver ran upstairs to his room once they got home, closed the door, and took the hat out of the bag. "Guess what? I'm going to take my black-belt exam next month!"

"Urggh," the hat said, shaking itself out. "What? I was fast asleep, and then . . ."

"Oh, sorry," Oliver said. "I'm just really psyched. Master T said I could take the exam next month, and . . ."

"This is the martial art of which you spoke?" the hat said, seeming more awake. "Ah, well, congratulations, Oliver. That is most delightful. And as I was saying, Patrick Henry?"

"Yes," Oliver said, and he put the hat on his head. And then he blinked and felt slightly dizzy, and all of a sudden he found himself in the doorway of a large assembly-type room. Men in fancy jackets and knee-length pants were standing in groups, waving their arms around and talking loudly. Next to him was a very tall young man with reddish hair who was also peering through the doorway. Thomas Jefferson? It had to be.

"Hello," Thomas Jefferson said. "You look somewhat familiar." And he assumed a puzzled look.

"I'm Oliver," Oliver said. "We met a while back. With Dabney Carr. Your friend."

"Ah, yes," Thomas Jefferson said, his face clearing. "Yes, I do remember."

Oliver realized that Thomas Jefferson must be several years older than he had been the last time Oliver had seen him, and Oliver wasn't older at all. But Thomas Jefferson seemed completely unfazed.

"My friend Patrick Henry is about to speak," Thomas Jefferson said excitedly. "You are aware, of course, of the Stamp Act? He is to speak in opposition to what the British Parliament has done. He has been elected to the House of Burgesses, you know."

Oliver reflected. The Stamp Act, he knew, involved taxes that the British had levied against the colonists. He was trying to remember what year that had happened. Sometime in the mid-1760s, he thought. 1765? So how old would Thomas Jefferson be now? Early twenties?

"Are you in the House of Burgesses too?" Oliver inquired. He knew Thomas Jefferson had been elected at some point, but it probably was later.

"Oh, no," Thomas Jefferson said, looking a little embarrassed. "Perhaps some time in the future, but for now, no. I am still a student."

"But are you . . . ?" Oliver began. He wanted to find out about Monticello. Had Thomas Jefferson started building it yet? And maybe he could ask him about some other things too.

But then someone started speaking. "'Tis Patrick Henry," Thomas Jefferson whispered to Oliver. "We must listen."

Patrick Henry was really into whatever it was he was saying. He was going on about Caesar and about Cromwell, and Oliver was trying to remember things about them both. Julius Caesar, maybe? The Roman emperor? And he knew that Cromwell was someone in English history, back in the 1600s, because his name had been Oliver Cromwell, and Oliver always liked to read up on famous Olivers. But he wasn't following the speech too well, he had to admit.

When Patrick Henry stopped speaking, a great hubbub arose from the men in the chamber. Some seemed to be applauding his words, while Oliver could also hear the word "treason" coming from somewhere in the room.

Thomas Jefferson looked awestruck. "What a speech," he exclaimed. "Most impressive. I find that listening to the words of Patrick Henry is similar to reading the words of Homer." Homer, Oliver knew, was a writer from ancient Greece who had written *The Odyssey*. But what did that have to do with the Stamp Act? He was confused.

"What does that . . . ?" Oliver began. His head itched, so he took off the hat. And suddenly, Thomas Jefferson, Patrick Henry, and the room of men vanished. He was in his bedroom.

"Oh, no," he said out loud. He hadn't had a chance to ask Thomas Jefferson about anything.

"Oliver, Oliver," the hat said. "The rules! I must remain . . ."

"On my head," Oliver said. "Will I get another chance?"

The hat seemed to nod.

Chapter ~4~

"We're starting a new tradition here at Eastview," Ms. Martin was saying. "Every time we have a new student coming into our class, we'll appoint someone as an Eastview Ambassador. Someone to welcome the new student and make them feel at home. Answer questions for them about anything that might seem confusing."

That sounded good, Oliver thought. He wished there had been an Eastview Ambassador last April. He still could use an Eastview Ambassador now, six months later. He usually felt as if he had no clue about what was going on. Pretty much everything seemed confusing.

"So today we're welcoming two new students!" Ms. Martin said enthusiastically. "Welcome to Colin and Rhiannon!"

Oliver, along with everyone else in the class, turned to look at Colin and Rhiannon, who were sitting at two new desks that had been added to Oliver's group of seats. Colin smiled and waved, and Rhiannon nodded solemnly. Neither of them, Oliver noticed, looked particularly nervous. He remembered his own first day. He had been literally shaking.

"And our Eastview Ambassador is Oliver!" Ms. Martin exclaimed.

"Oliver?" Tom blurted out. "But he's the new kid! He doesn't know anything!"

Oliver didn't even bother to feel insulted. He completely agreed. He didn't know anything. Why on earth had Ms. Martin chosen him?

"Why can't there be two Eastview Ambassadors?" Ava's best friend, Samantha, asked. "There's two new kids. I'd like to be an Eastview Ambassador."

A few other kids joined in, expressing their interest in being an Eastview Ambassador or their disbelief that Oliver had been selected. Or both.

"Thanks, Samantha," Ms. Martin said. "If you'd like to help out, that's a great idea. But I think Oliver can handle it." And she gave him a reassuring smile. "And now I thought we'd start the day with a welcome circle. I'd like to go around the room and have everyone say their name and something about themselves. Why don't we all stand up now."

As everyone got to their feet, Oliver thought he should say something privately to Colin and Rhiannon. Tell them that he would do his best, but he really didn't know that much. Tell them he was probably the worst person for the job. "So, like, I'm kind of new myself, and . . . ," he began.

"Hey, dude, don't worry about it," Colin said. "We'll be fine. So will you. Okay?" And he punched Oliver in the arm reassuringly.

"Yeah, okay," Oliver said, moving toward the circle that was forming around the room. Colin and Rhiannon followed him.

"Why don't we start with Ava," Ms. Martin said, "and go around from there."

Ava introduced herself and said something about how she was writing a short story about a girl

whose clarinet came to life and took her back in time to meet Mozart. Samantha, next to her, told everyone that she was going with her family to China next summer to meet some relatives she'd never met before. Tom said he was the best pitcher on his baseball team, causing laughs and snickers from Ryan, who said actually he, Ryan, was the best pitcher. Andrew said something about looking forward to going to a Wizards game and a Caps game soon, and Sam said he wanted to study ventriloquism.

As other kids said things about themselves, Oliver felt at a loss. What could he possibly say about himself? That he was new? He usually ended up saying something that everyone thought was weird, so lately he had been keeping quiet. Oh, maybe something about Tae Kwon Do! That would be good.

"Oliver?" Ms. Martin was saying. "Your turn!"

"I'm going to take my black-belt exam in Tae Kwon Do next month," he said.

Katie smiled at him, as did a few other kids, much to his surprise.

"Wonderful!" Ms. Martin said. "And Colin?" She looked at Colin, who was standing next to Oliver.

"Well, I guess I could say I was the best pitcher on my baseball team too, but that would probably not be cool since I'm the new kid," Colin said, and everyone laughed. Not at him, as they tended to do with Oliver, but with him. "I'm Colin, and we've just moved here from Spain," he said. "We've moved a lot, so we're pretty much always the new kids. But so it goes." And he smiled at everyone. They all smiled back, except Tom and Ryan, who were whispering to each other and looked kind of upset.

Clearly Colin had social skills, Oliver thought. He wondered why some people had them and some people— like himself, no matter what Cassie said—just didn't.

"I'm Rhiannon," Rhiannon was saying. "Colin's twin sister. I understand you've been studying the American Revolution. We were at an American school in Spain, so we studied some of that too, plus I've done a lot of reading on my own, so I think I'll be prepared. I did a project on the Bill of Rights, focusing in particular on the First Amendment. I'm also particularly interested in Thomas Jefferson and his scientific inventions. Did you know that he slept in a bed that was placed in a special alcove?"

Oliver did know, and, he assumed, so did the whole class because he had told them about it just the other day. If they had been listening, that is.

"Wow, she sounds like a girl version of Oliver," Tom said loudly, causing a few kids to laugh. "Another brainiac."

She kind of did. Oliver wasn't sure what to make of that.

"Settle down, everyone," Ms. Martin said. "And Tom, that's enough. So why don't you all go back to your seats now, and we'll start on the science lesson about hydroponics."

Oliver already understood pretty much everything about hydroponics, because he'd done a lot of extra reading, so he found his mind wandering as his table group made its way over to their plant and started taking notes and discussing how much the plant had grown.

He really should discuss hydroponics with Thomas Jefferson, he thought. Thomas Jefferson probably would have some ideas about it, given that he was into farming, and thus presumably had an interest in plants and how they grow. Maybe Madison Hemings would be interested too. Would the hat take him back again? Maybe after school? Would it just be him this time, or would it insist on bringing his sisters?

". . . right, Oliver?" It was Ms. Martin, who was standing next to him and giving him an inquiring look.

"Uh-huh," he managed, not sure what he was agreeing to.

"I've already studied this," Rhiannon said. "I did some extra science work last year and grew some plants in water at home as a science fair project. Colin helped me. We won a special award."

They both nodded. The other kids in the group—Katie, Samantha, and Andrew—looked impressed.

"Fantastic!" Ms. Martin said. "But I'm sure Oliver will

be able to answer any questions you might have. And you all know that the science fair is coming up in December. I'll be talking some more about that later today."

Oliver had forgotten. The idea of a science fair without Jarlo was too much to contemplate. How could he do the cow project by himself? It was kind of complicated. And he knew if he asked anyone in his class, even Sam, they'd all think it was bizarre. They wouldn't want to work with him. They all had people to work with, anyway. Friends. He sighed.

His mind continued to drift along as the class moved from science to math, and then to lunch.

"So what's the deal with the cafeteria?" Colin asked Oliver, as the class filed down to the cafeteria. "Like, who do you usually eat with?"

Usually Oliver ate by himself, or maybe sometimes with Sam. Or occasionally with Ava and Samantha, or maybe Katie. She had played Martha Washington when Oliver had played George, so he had sometimes rehearsed with her. Once again, he felt he was completely miscast as Eastview Ambassador. Pretty much anyone else would have been a better guide. "Oh, it depends," he said, hoping he sounded slightly mysterious rather than just pitiful.

Colin and Rhiannon sat down on either side of Oliver and pulled out their lunch boxes. "Turkey again," Colin said. "My mum's been on a big kick with turkey lately. Very American. I mean, my mom."

"I think Oliver knows that we're part British," Rhiannon said. "You don't need to translate into American for him."

Oliver nodded. He was aware that kids in Britain tended to say "mum" instead of "mom."

"Yeah, I do end up translating a lot," Colin said. "A lot of kids here in the States don't seem to always get what we're saying. But lately I just try to avoid saying anything that sounds British or might be confusing."

As the three of them ate, Oliver looked around the room. Ryan and Tom were sitting at a table with a bunch of other boys. Probably planning what they would play at recess today. Sam was at that table, which was surprising. In fact, Ryan was sitting next to Sam and seemed to be focusing on him. Talking to him as if he were explaining something to him. Oliver wondered why. Even he knew that Ryan and Sam weren't especially friendly.

"So those two dudes over there?" Colin asked, gesturing over toward Ryan and Tom. "They sort of run things, like, sports and all? At least, that's what it seems like."

"Yeah," Oliver said.

"I assume girls are included?" Rhiannon said. "At some of our schools, most of the girls weren't, except me."

Oliver thought. He wasn't sure. He hadn't really paid much attention to what the girls were, or weren't, doing at recess. "I don't think so," he concluded. "I mean, occasionally Katie joins in, but usually not."

"I'm going to change that," Rhiannon said. "That's ridiculous."

"Go for it, R.," Colin said, and the two of them smiled at each other. And also at Oliver.

"Yeah," Oliver said, smiling back at the two of them.

It did seem ridiculous, now that he thought about it. He remembered Ruby complaining about being excluded from the boys' games at recess back when she was his age, and how she used to protest. "My sister Ruby would agree."

"She's cool," Colin said. "We liked her."

Rhiannon nodded.

Really? Oliver wasn't sure what the right response was to that. "I despise her" did not seem appropriate, somehow. So he remained silent.

Just then, the lunch monitors blew the whistle for everyone to pack up and head out to recess. Oliver looked at Colin and Rhiannon. "Recess," he said. "We have to put our lunch boxes in the bin over there."

As they deposited their lunch boxes and followed the other kids out to the field, Oliver observed that Ryan and Tom were, as usual, dividing the boys up into teams.

"No, it's soccer today," Tom was saying to Andrew. "We played kickball yesterday, okay?"

"Football?" Colin said. "I mean, soccer? Cool!" He picked up a stray soccer ball and started passing it back and forth to Rhiannon. They both apparently were incredibly talented at soccer, too, in addition to basketball, Oliver thought to himself. As the two of them continued showing off various soccer moves, the group of boys gathered around them to watch. Ryan and Tom were standing by themselves, muttering to each other and looking even more upset than they had during class.

"Hey, let's let the new kids be the captains today," said James, one of Tom and Ryan's usual followers. "They're, like, super-skilled at soccer."

"Yeah," Oliver found himself agreeing, only to be met with glares from Tom and Ryan.

"What the . . ." Tom said. "I mean, we're always the captains."

"No problem," Colin said, kicking the ball over to Tom. "You go ahead. But thanks anyway," and he looked at James and Oliver.

"Well, I want you on my team," Tom said to Colin. "You can have her," and he looked between Ryan and Rhiannon.

"Fine," Ryan said. "So let's go, dudes." He looked at Rhiannon. "And dudette."

"I'm fine either way," Rhiannon said. "Dude, dudette, whatever. Just so I can play."

Katie approached the group. "I'm in too," she said. "Rhiannon, can I be on your team?"

Ryan and Rhiannon both nodded, and the game soon began. Oliver had been assigned to Tom's team. As usual, Oliver wasn't the absolute worst player, but he certainly wasn't the best. Ryan seemed to be spending a lot of time passing the ball to Sam, and shouting instructions to Sam, who, Oliver noticed, was playing a little better than usual. Generally, Sam was about at Oliver's level, if not a little worse. Colin and Rhiannon had each scored three goals when Oliver heard the whistle blow signaling the end of recess.

A crowd of kids clustered around Colin and Rhiannon as the group made its way back to class.

Oliver ended up next to Sam. "Wow, they're really good," Sam said, as they went up the stairway to Ms. Martin's classroom. Sam looked completely out of breath but happier than usual.

"Yeah, I know," Oliver said. "You should see them play basketball."

"So how's the hat doing?" Sam asked, almost whispering. "I mean, has it . . ."

"I was standing with Thomas Jefferson watching Patrick Henry give a speech in the Virginia House of Burgesses," Oliver whispered back. "I think it was in 1765 or so. About the Stamp Act. But that's it so far. I was hoping maybe later today it would do something."

"Maybe I could come along?" Sam inquired.

Oliver nodded. And the two of them entered the classroom, where Ms. Martin was writing something on the whiteboard.

"Science Fair," she wrote.

Oliver felt a pang, thinking of Jarlo. Thinking of them working with Arun on what had been Oliver's project. Thinking of his school in New Jersey and his house and how easy everything had been. And how he had probably never appreciated it enough.

"The science fair will be in December," Ms. Martin said. "I've given you each a worksheet with information I'd like you to fill in and return by Friday. If you change your mind about your project and who you'd like to work with, that's fine, but this will get you started. And you can always work on your own."

All the kids started talking at once, as Ms. Martin continued writing information on the board. Except Oliver. A month ago, he would have started discussing his project. Expounding upon the details of farting cows. Regardless of whether anyone really cared about it. But what was the point? They'd all just laugh.

Maybe he should just forget about farting cows, he thought. Maybe he could bring Sam's hat in and do a project on time travel. Maybe the hat would help him figure the whole thing out and he'd become famous. Maybe . . .

". . . Oliver?"

Ms. Martin was looking at him, and the class had fallen silent.

Oliver blinked and glanced over at her. What had he missed now?

"I thought you could explain what we've been doing in reading," Ms. Martin said.

Oh, of course. The class had been reading various tall tales, including the story of Paul Bunyan. Oliver had done some extra work and had learned a great deal about the legend of Paul Bunyan, the larger-than-life lumberman.

"Did you know that the first stories about Paul Bunyan were published in 1910?" Oliver began. "Did you know that the poet Robert Frost wrote about him? Did you know . . ."

"Oh, jeez," he could hear Tom whispering. "There he goes again."

Oliver stopped. What had he said that was wrong this time? Those were interesting facts, weren't they?

"Tom, enough," Ms. Martin said, frowning. "Please. And Oliver, thank you. Yes, we've been reading tall tales, including the legend of Paul Bunyan. Colin and Rhiannon, I'll give you copies of the book we've been using, okay?"

And the class started discussing Paul Bunyan, and

then they discussed the paper they would start writing the next day about tall tales, and then Oliver found himself on the bus heading home. He was sitting in a group with Sam, Colin, and Rhiannon, which was unusual given that he usually ended up sitting by himself, or sometimes with some random kid he didn't really know if the bus was crowded that day.

The four of them got off the bus together and then split up to head to their respective houses. Sam, however, followed along with Oliver. Oh yeah, Oliver remembered. The hat. He wondered what would happen this time. If the hat would cooperate and take them somewhere. And not take Ruby, or even Cassie, along.

But when he and Sam arrived at his house, neither Ruby nor Cassie was home, much to Oliver's surprise. Usually they were home and were responsible for taking him to Tae Kwon Do or anything else he might need to attend that didn't require driving. Cassie had only just gotten her license, and their parents didn't want her driving anyone else.

Instead, when the door to his house opened, he saw a young woman with a round face and curly hair who looked slightly familiar. She appeared to be a little older than Cassie.

"Celia!" Sam exclaimed, looking surprised. "What are you doing here?"

Oh, that's right. Oliver remembered now. His sisters had complained that they had after-school activities and other plans, and someone else should take over the responsibility for Oliver. So his mom had asked around, and it turned out that Celia, a friend of Sam's cousin

Nigel from college—or maybe she was his girlfriend, Sam wasn't sure—was looking for extra work. And here she was. He had met her once but had completely forgotten about her new role in his life.

"Sam!" Celia said, smiling happily. "And Oliver! So Oliver, I need to take you to Tae Kwon Do now, okay? Sam, I guess you'll have to go back to your house. I know Nigel's there."

"But . . ." Sam began, looking disappointed.

"Maybe you can come back later," Oliver said. "Sorry about that." He was sorry, too, to have to postpone the hat adventure. Although, at the same time, he was excited about going to Tae Kwon Do now that he might get his black belt in the near future.

Sam departed, trudging back up the street, and Oliver and Celia headed to the studio. Celia spent most of the way there talking about how she had made it to blue belt and had stopped, but maybe she'd start again, and how did he like it, and did he like living here, and how had it been living in New Jersey? She talked a lot, Oliver realized. And she talked all the way home from Tae Kwon Do too. He finally was able to get away and upstairs to the hat.

"I have a wonderful adventure in store for you, Oliver!" the hat announced, bouncing up and down as Oliver put it on his head. "You know, of course, about the Declaration of Independence. That Mr. Jefferson wrote the Declaration, with the help of Mr. Adams and Dr. Franklin and some others, yes? In Philadelphia, in the year 1776?"

"Yes!" Oliver said. This was amazing! Would he get

to see Thomas Jefferson writing the Declaration of Independence? Would he get to meet John Adams and Benjamin Franklin? The dizzy feeling swept over him, and in the midst of it he remembered Sam. He really should have invited him along. But then he opened his eyes, and Sam went completely out of his thoughts.

Oliver was standing in a smallish room. A man was seated at a table, his head in his hands and his shirtsleeves rolled up. Large sheets of paper were strewn across the table's surface, with scribbled writing, much of it crossed out, on them. Also on the table lay a wooden board of sorts, propped open, with more papers on it, and a pen. Oliver looked closer. The man appeared, indeed, to be Thomas Jefferson. But what was he doing? Were those scribbled sheets of paper the Declaration of Independence?

Thomas Jefferson groaned and lifted his head from his hands. He peered blearily at Oliver. "Oh, my young friend. You have returned." He frowned. "But not at an auspicious moment, I fear. This document is driving me to distraction." And he gestured at the sheets of paper on the desk. "I wrote and wrote. I worked and worked. Mr. Adams and Dr. Franklin worked and worked. And then today we presented it to the gathering."

He stood up and started pacing around the room. It was kind of hot, and Thomas Jefferson pulled out a handkerchief and wiped his brow. "And one criticism on another was heaped upon it! The gentlemen from the North! The gentlemen from the South! And I had to sit there and listen to all of this! I tried to remain silent, for I did not wish to show how upset I felt. Do you know what it is like to work so hard, so diligently, on something, and no appreciation is shown? Only criticism?"

He stopped pacing, and his eyes bored into Oliver's as he looked down at him.

Oliver tried to think. Well, yes! There had been the time in fourth grade when he and Jarlo had presented a huge Lego diorama to the class, meant to display a set of stores in the main street of their town. It had been a project on local businesses, he remembered. They had worked incredibly hard on it. But no one had seemed at all impressed by it. Another group of kids had done an even-bigger Lego diorama, and that had received all the attention. All the praise. Jared had acted all cool about it, like the lack of attention was no big deal, but Oliver and Arlo had been upset. Not that his problems compared with Thomas Jefferson's, of course. A Lego diorama was hardly the Declaration of Independence. But still. He nodded.

"Well, then you must understand how I feel at this moment," Thomas Jefferson continued. "I wanted to express my support in the document for the end of slavery, but the gentlemen from various southern states would not go along with that, so out it went."

"What?" Oliver said, surprised. "But you have slaves."

"Yes, but I believe the system is no good," Thomas Jefferson said. "I have said that before. Though I do own slaves; that is true."

"How can you own slaves if you think the system is no good?" Oliver inquired. Finally. He was getting to the heart of the matter. "That doesn't make sense."

"Well, maybe not," Thomas Jefferson said. "It is hard to explain. I believe that the system should end. But I do have my responsibilities. To all the people at Monticello. To my family. My dependents."

Oliver felt more confused than ever.

"And now I must rewrite this and rewrite that, and eliminate some of the material I thought was the most promising," Thomas Jefferson was continuing, running his hands through his hair. "We have voted today on independence from Britain, which is of course a huge step to take, but the document itself cannot be approved until these changes are made." He sat back down at his desk and picked up the pen.

"Can I see?" Oliver said, leaning over the table to look more closely at the papers. He managed to get a glimpse of a line that looked like "We hold these truths to be self-evident."

"Self-evident," Thomas Jefferson said, pointing the pen at the paper. "A good word, do you not agree? Dr. Franklin's suggestion."

"Are they coming over here? John Adams and Benjamin Franklin, I mean?" Oliver asked. He'd really like to meet them. "Like, to help you finish up?"

"I believe so, yes," Thomas Jefferson said, nodding. "But I do not know exactly when."

Oliver again noticed the wooden platform resting on the table. "What's this?" he asked, curious.

"It is a portable desk," Thomas Jefferson said. "Of my own design. I can take it with me and use it propped at a certain angle to make it comfortable for writing. And it has a drawer on the side, you see?" He put the pen down and pulled the drawer open. "For storage."

"Cool," Oliver said. He'd like to have one of those himself. Maybe use it for homework or something. "So are there any other portable desks around?" Maybe he could figure out a way to bring one of them back with him. Although wouldn't that be messing with the space-time continuum or whatever?

"No, not as far as I know," Thomas Jefferson replied. He looked preoccupied and picked up the pen again.

Oliver was feeling kind of hot and sweaty, so he took off the hat to wipe his forehead, and of course a minute later Thomas Jefferson, the Declaration of Independence, the portable desk, the pen, and the room were gone.

Instead, he was in his own room. The hat seemed to be shaking its head reproachfully at him.

Chapter

~5~

The next day, Oliver woke up hoping the hat would talk to him about their next adventure. But it was snoring gently in its Mount Vernon bag and seemed disinclined to participate in any conversation—although Oliver tried talking to it for an hour or so before he had to go to school.

But three interesting things did happen that day. To begin with, at school, Colin and Rhiannon seemed to be attracting a bigger and bigger crowd of admirers. At recess, Tom and Ryan declared that everyone would play kickball, and Colin and Rhiannon turned out to be as talented at kickball as they were at every other sport. But despite all the admirers, they stuck close to Oliver. They ate with him at lunch, they included him in the kickball game, and they sat with him on the bus.

Which was good, because a second thing had happened. Involving Sam. At the bus stop that morning, Sam had approached Oliver, looking concerned.

"So did you go anywhere yesterday?" Sam asked, pulling Oliver to the side so Colin and Rhiannon and the other kids couldn't hear. "With the hat?"

"Go anywhere yesterday?"

Oliver suddenly remembered. He hadn't invited Sam to come along. Oh, shoot. He really should have. But it had all taken place so quickly. Still, he should have invited Sam as soon as he got home. He sighed.

"Did you travel back?" Sam persisted. "I mean, did you see Thomas Jefferson again?"

Oliver nodded weakly, not sure what to say.

"Oh," Sam said, and he turned and walked away.

This definitely wasn't good, Oliver realized. Sam was one of the only people who would talk to him, and now Sam was mad at him, understandably enough. So Sam wasn't talking to him, Jared and Arlo weren't really interested in talking to him anymore, and most of the other kids didn't seem to care about him one way or the other. It was discouraging.

One person, though, did seem unusually interested in talking to him—Ruby. That was the third interesting thing that had happened that day. Instead of arguing with him and criticizing him, she was being super-nice.

"Hey, Olls, you want me to play that new Xbox game with you now?" Ruby said after dinner. Usually she scorned his video games.

"Well, yeah," Oliver said, surprised. "Okay."

They went down to the basement and played for a while, and then she started asking him about the new kids, and about Sam, and he started telling her various things about them, and she said Nico was in her English class and had told her he was interested in the newspaper too, and Oliver said that was cool, and the two of them seemed to be having a pretty normal conversation for once.

"So how's the hat?" Ruby asked, her eyes narrowing, after the normal conversation had been going on for some time.

Oh. She was being nice because she wanted something from him. She wanted to go back and meet Thomas Jefferson again. Obviously. Oliver smacked his forehead. Duh! Why hadn't he figured that out sooner?

"Fine," he replied.

"Has it taken you anywhere else?" she asked.

"Yeah," he said. He really didn't want to say anything more.

"Come on, Olls," she wheedled. "Where? Who did you meet?"

"Maybe I'll tell you another time," Oliver said, and he left the basement and went back upstairs. How had he been so gullible?

He found the hat, still in the bag. "Sisters," he muttered,

hoping the hat would hear him and offer words of wisdom. But it was still asleep.

His mom's iPad was in his room—she hardly used it—and he decided to look up Madison Hemings. Find out more about him. He knew Madison Hemings had written about his life, and he wondered if it was available online.

He googled Madison Hemings, and there it was. A long article that Madison Hemings had written in something called the *Pike County Republican* in 1873. Was that a newspaper? It was too bad Ruby was so annoying, because she would know the answer to that. But he didn't really feel like asking her.

The article started by describing Madison Hemings's great-grandmother and great-grandfather, and Oliver skimmed through the early paragraphs, hoping to learn more about Madison himself.

But before he could get too far, the hat started stirring in its bag. It seemed to stretch and yawn. "Aaaahhhh," it said. "Such a wonderful nap! Please remove me from the bag, Oliver."

Oliver did so, feeling a surge of anticipation. "So are we going somewhere?" he asked, putting the hat on his head.

"Madison Hemings?" the hat said. Could it read? How fascinating.

"Can you read?" Oliver inquired.

"Never you mind what I can or cannot do," the hat said. "We hats can do many things that you humans would never imagine." It sniffed in a self-satisfied way. "'The moment a person forms a theory, his imagination sees in every object only the traits which favor that theory.' Another quote from Mr. Jefferson."

"So, you mean, I'm assuming hats can only sit on someone's head, but they can really do more?"

"That, my dear Oliver, is self-evident," the hat said. "A word I'm sure you're familiar with."

Oliver nodded, and then he felt the dizzy feeling, and then he was standing outside Monticello again. It was a hot day, and the sun was high in the sky. The white pillars glistened. Various people were rushing about, intent on their tasks, and suddenly someone was next to him.

He glanced over and wasn't entirely surprised to find Madison Hemings. He was holding a pile of what looked like laundry.

"Oh, it is you again," Madison Hemings said, smiling. "You disappeared so quickly the other time, I had no idea I would see you once more. Come, walk with me to that cabin, for I must deliver this."

Oliver agreed, and they walked side by side for a few minutes. Madison Hemings looked about the same age that he had the last time. Which meant Oliver was back in approximately 1815. Thomas Jefferson, whom Oliver had last seen as a man in his early thirties writing the Declaration of Independence, must be . . . Oliver calculated quickly . . . in his early seventies. This was almost forty years later.

But Oliver saw no sign of Thomas Jefferson. Everyone around him seemed to be working hard at whatever task they were doing. Even the kids his own age.

"Do you go to school?" Oliver asked.

"Oh, no," Madison Hemings said. His voice dropped to a whisper. "But the Jefferson grandchildren have taught me a bit here and there, so I am able to read and write."

But Madison Hemings was actually a Jefferson too, Oliver thought.

"When I am slightly older I shall most likely learn the trade of carpenter," Madison Hemings continued. "My uncle is a skilled carpenter, and I believe I am to be working with him. I feel it is important to learn a trade. For now, I help with various tasks. My sister and brothers and I are perhaps asked to do less than many other people here at Monticello, for which I suppose I should be glad." Although, understandably, he didn't look especially glad. Madison Hemings still wasn't free, after all. He hadn't been freed until he was an adult, Oliver knew. Sally Hemings, his mother, had never been freed.

Oliver wished he had read more of Madison Hemings's story, to be able to ask more questions. "So were you born here?"

"Oh, yes," Madison Hemings said. "The story has it that I was named by Mrs. Madison. She asked my mother to name me Madison and promised my mother a gift were she to agree. Sadly, the gift was never given."

"You mean Dolley Madison?" Oliver asked. "James

Madison's wife? James Madison, like, the fourth president?" He tried thinking about who was president in 1817, but came up blank. Would it still be James Madison, or had he already finished being president? Oliver knew he had been president after Thomas Jefferson, and that the two of them were good friends.

"That's right," Madison Hemings said. "My full name is James Madison Hemings, but I do not use the James."

They had stopped in front of one of the cabins, and Madison Hemings darted inside with the pile of laundry, or whatever it was, and Oliver was left standing outside.

He gazed up at the house, where he assumed Thomas Jefferson probably was sitting in that study, writing something. Or maybe inventing something. He should ask Thomas Jefferson about the science fair project. Maybe he'd have a good idea about something Oliver could do, assuming the cow idea didn't end up happening.

Madison Hemings reappeared. "You know, Oliver, you were going to show me the hat," he said. "Remember?"

"Oh, yeah," Oliver said. "You're right, I was." And unthinkingly, he took off the hat.

And he was back in his room. Of course. Would he ever learn?

"Really, Oliver!" the hat said. "I know you meant to be kind, but I must, absolutely must, stay on your head. Well, there's always another time."

And it seemed to fall asleep.

Oliver put it back in its bag and determined that perhaps he should go to sleep himself. Before he knew it, it was the next morning. He had fallen asleep in his clothes. His mother, or someone, must have pulled the

covers up and basically tucked him in. He looked at the iPad and determined that it was almost time for him to leave for the bus. What had become of everyone?

He opened his door and looked around. Why hadn't anyone woken him up? Descending the stairs and approaching the kitchen, he spotted his mom, sipping some coffee and checking something on her phone. She was in her work clothes.

"Oh, good," she said, sounding relieved and giving him a hug. "I was about to wake you. You just seemed so tired, I thought I'd let you sleep a little more."

Time travel was exhausting, Oliver thought, as he helped himself to some cereal. But of course he couldn't tell her that. And he really had to hurry up, or he'd miss the bus.

Sam ignored him on the bus and ignored him on the way out of the bus to the classroom and ignored him in the classroom too. The very sight of Sam made Oliver feel even more guilty. Not only had he not invited Sam along to see Thomas Jefferson writing the Declaration of Independence, he also hadn't invited him to meet Madison Hemings. But what could he do about it now? Probably nothing, he concluded.

In class, Ms. Martin asked them to discuss their science fair ideas with their table groups, and Oliver found himself describing the cow project to Colin, Rhiannon, Katie, Samantha, and Andrew, who all seemed sort of fascinated.

"But of course I can't do that project, because Jared and Arlo are back in New Jersey," Oliver concluded. "They're twins, just like you guys," and he gestured at Colin and Rhiannon. "Except they're identical, and they're both boys."

"Well, why can't you do it with us?" Rhiannon asked. "It sounds like a cool project, even if you can't do it with your friends in New Jersey. And of course they don't just fart, they burp too."

"Who burps?" Oliver asked, slightly confused. Jared and Arlo?

"The cows," Rhiannon said. "The gas comes out when they burp too."

"Right," Oliver said. Of course, he knew that already. But how did she know it? Was she a secret expert on gassy cows? She did seem to know about an awful lot of things.

So they all kept talking about cows, and it turned out Rhiannon knew almost as much as Oliver about them, and then the rest of the day seemed to pass by quickly, and then it was time for the after-school chess club.

Oliver enjoyed the chess club. But today he felt a little uneasy because Sam was in the chess club too. And Sam still wasn't speaking to him. Fortunately, Mr. Alexander, the chess club teacher, assigned Oliver to play with Ben, a fourth-grader who was pretty good at chess, and Sam to play against Ryan. It had surprised Oliver when Ryan joined the chess club a few weeks earlier. He didn't really seem like the chess club type. But since then, he hadn't missed a meeting. And he seemed to be good at it.

Oliver really would have to invite Sam along the next time the hat took him on an adventure, he thought. This was not a good situation. And it got even more awkward when Celia and Nigel showed up in Celia's car to pick Oliver and Sam up after the chess club meeting ended. The two of them were stuck sitting together in the backseat, neither of them saying a word.

Celia talked all the way home, so it wasn't totally obvious that Sam and Oliver were at odds. And once Oliver was back in his room, he really didn't feel like inviting Sam along if the hat chose to take Oliver somewhere. The hat was his for the week, wasn't it? Why would Sam have to come along, anyway?

He reached for the hat and set it gently on his bed. "Are you awake?" he inquired.

Clearly it was, because it started speaking excitedly. "Did you know that Thomas Jefferson was a US representative in Paris after the Revolutionary War ended? Along with Mr. Adams, of course. And he and both Mr. and Mrs. Adams became quite friendly. Of course, Mrs. Jefferson had recently passed away, which was a deep sorrow for Mr. Jefferson and their daughters." And the hat seemed to look very sad.

Oliver had known that. It was incredibly sad, yes.

"Well?" the hat said.

"Okay," Oliver said, and put the hat on his head and closed his eyes once the dizzy feeling hit.

He opened his eyes to find himself in what appeared to be a garden, next to a gigantic house. He was walking along a path with several people. Glancing at them, he realized that one of them was Thomas Jefferson. He looked older than he had the last time. Sort of middle-aged. Thomas Jefferson was engaged in conversation with two familiar-looking people. Were they John and Abigail Adams? Oliver thought so. And there were two younger people, maybe about Cassie's age, or Celia's, one boy and one girl. Behind the group trailed a couple of men. Were they servants of some kind?

"Ah, Oliver," Thomas Jefferson said, noticing him. "A pleasure as always. You of course are familiar with Mr. and Mrs. Adams, and their children Nabby and John Quincy?"

Cool! "Yeah," Oliver said. "I mean, yes, good to meet you." He really should try to be more polite, given that he was in the company of three future presidents—the two Adamses and Thomas Jefferson—and one future first lady.

"Shall we sit?" Abigail Adams said, gesturing at a small table filled with food. "Mr. Jefferson?," and she beckoned to Thomas Jefferson.

"Why, thank you!" Thomas Jefferson said, sitting down next to Abigail Adams. Oliver hovered behind

Thomas Jefferson, not sure if he should take a seat too. After all, they hadn't exactly expected him. The table was set for five.

All of a sudden, to Oliver's complete shock, J.P. came running out from behind a nearby bush toward the table, Ava behind him. What on earth were they doing here? J.P. was holding a bobblehead that looked like John Adams. Okay, this was all just getting too weird.

One of the servants had brought over a chair for Oliver, and he collapsed into it, next to Thomas Jefferson. Was he hallucinating?

"It's Ava and J.P.!" Nabby Adams said, not seeming especially surprised. As if she knew them quite well. "My goodness, it's been so long!"

"Hello, Nabby, John Quincy, Mr. and Mrs. Adams, Mr. Jefferson." Ava rattled them all off. "It's great to see you again!"

Why hadn't she said hello to him too? Oliver wondered.

Surely she saw him sitting there. Wouldn't she be surprised to see him? Wouldn't she notice that he, too, was back in the eighteenth century? What was going on, anyway?

"Bonjour!" J.P. said, and proceeded to say some things in what Oliver assumed was French. That's right, he was bilingual, Oliver remembered.

"And you still have the toy that resembles Father," John Quincy Adams said, looking at J.P.'s bobblehead.

J.P. smacked his forehead. "Yes, and we keep forgetting to bring you the second one."

Oliver thought to himself: Could the bobblehead be sort of like the hat? Something that took J.P. and Ava back and forth in time? What else had they seen? Clearly this was far from the first time they'd visited with the Adamses.

But why didn't they notice him? That was extremely puzzling.

"Please, join us," Abigail Adams said to Ava and J.P. "We are still accustoming ourselves to this extremely large house and all the servants! And this wonderful lawn!"

Ava and J.P. sat down on two more chairs provided by the servants and started eating. Oliver helped himself to some bread and pastries. They were really delicious. His mouth was so full he couldn't really participate in the conversation.

"Mr. Jefferson was just telling us of some of his latest purchases," Abigail Adams said.

"Yes, new fancy French clothes, wine, even a new sword," John Adams added.

Thomas Jefferson smiled faintly and nodded. "All true," he said. "And more books too."

"So can I see it?" J.P. asked.

"See what?" Thomas Jefferson replied, seeming puzzled.

"The sword!" J.P. said. "Obviously!"

"Ah, well, the sword is only for use with certain clothes," Thomas Jefferson said. "But perhaps you can see it another time. We could make use of you as an interpreter, perhaps, eh?" And he turned to John Adams.

"Excellent, yes," John Adams said. "My French has greatly improved, but I do not know that I would describe myself as completely fluent."

"And I certainly am not," Thomas Jefferson said.

"I am," J.P. said. "I'm bilingual!"

"We shall have to take you on, then, as our young interpreter," John Adams said, and ruffled J.P.'s hair as Abigail Adams smiled down at him.

"George wanted to use me as an interpreter too," J.P. continued. "George Washington. It was during some war or other. With the French. But it didn't work out."

"What a lively imagination," Abigail Adams said fondly.

This was all just too bizarre, Oliver thought. So J.P. actually had met George Washington? But why didn't Ava and J.P. seem to see him? He stood up and made his way over to the other side of the table, waving his arms at Ava and J.P.

"Hey, Ava!" he cried. "J.P.!" The Adamses and Thomas Jefferson were still busy discussing Thomas Jefferson's latest shopping trip—Oliver knew from his research that Thomas Jefferson tended to spend a lot of money on whatever he was interested in—so they weren't really paying attention to Oliver. "Don't you see me?"

But they didn't seem to. They were kind of blinking in his direction, but it was as if Oliver were completely invisible.

J.P. was showing the bobblehead to Thomas Jefferson, who was across the table from him. "It's John!" J.P. exclaimed. "See?"

"Extraordinary!" Thomas Jefferson said, taking the bobblehead and examining it closely. "Where did you come by this toy?"

"The John Adams Visitor Center," J.P. said happily.

Oh, Oliver thought. He knew they had gone to Boston a couple of weekends ago for someone's wedding. Maybe that's how they ended up with this connection to the Adams family—who were from the Boston area, he knew.

"You have a center for visitors?" Thomas Jefferson said, raising an eyebrow and looking over at John Adams.

"I suppose I do," John Adams said, looking pleased.

But still. Why weren't Ava and J.P. aware that he, Oliver, was on this same time-travel adventure? That they'd somehow bumped into each other back in 1780-something?

He waved his hands right in Ava's face. Surely she'd have to see him. But she didn't seem to. Neither did J.P. And suddenly, much to Oliver's astonishment, Ava and J.P. vanished.

"Oh my god!" he said, startled. Where had they gone?

"Well, they do tend to come and go rather suddenly," Nabby Adams said, shaking her head. "But they come back eventually." The other Adamses nodded.

"You know, you do the same thing," Thomas Jefferson said, looking at Oliver. "Most extraordinary. They seem to be friends of yours, am I correct?"

Friends? Oliver wasn't sure. "I live right near them," he said. But he wasn't really clear on how much more he should say. It might confuse them, even Thomas Jefferson with his great scientific mind.

"I do find your hat quite intriguing," Thomas Jefferson said. "The style is most distinctive. Might I take a look?"

Oliver sighed. He knew what would happen. But he couldn't exactly say no, could he? So he started to hand it over.

And he once again was back in his room.

"Well, this time there was nothing much you could do," the hat said. "Short of being rude to Mr. Jefferson in front of the Adams family, that is. So I understand." It preened itself a little. "I am most distinctive, yes, if I do say so myself." And it paused. "Might I offer a suggestion for the future?"

Oliver nodded.

"You might recall the quotation from Mr. Jefferson that I told you and Sam the other day," the hat continued. "Peace and friendship with all mankind is our wisest policy, and I wish we may be permitted to pursue it?"

"Yes," Oliver said.

"Just keep that in mind," the hat said.

Oliver wasn't sure what the hat was referring to. But he did know something he wanted to ask the hat about. "Why were Ava and J.P. back there?" he queried. "What was going on with that?"

But the only reply from the hat was a gentle snore.

Chapter
~6~

At the bus stop the next morning, Oliver closely observed Ava and J.P. They were standing together near the swings, sort of arguing but sort of laughing. He wondered if he should ask them about the bobblehead. About what they were doing hanging out with John and Abigail Adams and their kids. But they hadn't seen him back there. So they had no idea he had been there too. It was baffling. He probably should consult with the hat first.

Oliver was so busy watching Ava and J.P. that he was startled to find Sam standing next to him.

"Hey, Oliver," Sam said.

Oliver nodded at him, not sure what to say. "Hi."

"So I've been thinking," Sam said, looking around before continuing, to make sure no one was listening. "Like, this is your adventure. The hat wanted you to have it this week, not me. So I was kind of acting like a jerk. So, well, sorry."

Oliver was surprised. "Wow," he said. "Okay. But it's fine if you want to come along. As long as I have the hat, I mean." He was so relieved that Sam wasn't mad at him anymore that he blurted out, "Did you know I saw Ava and J.P. back in the eighteenth century?" Oh, no. He probably shouldn't have said that. Maybe it wasn't a good thing to reveal the time-travel adventures of others.

Sam's eyes widened. "What?" he said. "Ava and J.P.? But . . ."

"They had a bobblehead of John Adams with them," Oliver whispered. "Maybe it's kind of like the hat? It takes them back in time? But they didn't see me. It was really weird. I kept waving my hands around in their faces but, like, nothing. It was as if I wasn't there. But they seemed to be good friends with the whole Adams family."

"Weird, yeah," Sam muttered to himself. "I wonder how that would have happened. We'll have to ask the hat to explain."

"Yeah," Oliver said, and then the bus belched to a stop next to them and they had to end that particular conversation.

The rest of the school day passed by quickly, and Oliver came home to find both Ruby and Cassie at home. They were sprawled on the family room sofa, each tapping away at her phone, their backpacks on the floor.

"Where's Celia?" Oliver asked. Honestly, he'd rather see Celia than Ruby.

"Olls, really," Ruby said impatiently, putting her phone down. "Celia isn't coming today because Cassie and I don't have anything after school. Don't you remember?"

Well, he didn't. But okay. He headed for the kitchen, which opened onto the family room, to get a snack.

"Olls?" Ruby continued. "We all need to talk. Come

here and sit down."

This sounded less than promising. What exactly did Ruby feel the need to discuss?

"Ollie?" Cassie said. She set her phone on the coffee table and took a bite of an apple she was holding in her other hand. "Ruby told me something interesting about your hat. I mean, Sam's hat. And I'd like to participate too. It's not really fair that you and Ruby got to go meet Thomas Jefferson and I didn't. Especially if I actually get into UVA. I kind of want to ask him some stuff about the school, you know?"

Oliver felt his heart sink as he sat down on the armchair next to the sofa with his granola bar and some water. Why did the two of them need to interfere, anyway? This was his hat for the week. Not Sam's, and not his sisters'. At least Sam seemed to get it.

But on the other hand, he felt kind of bad for Cassie. Why shouldn't she get to come on an adventure, at least once?

"Yeah," he said, looking at Cassie. "I know. You probably should get to try it out once." He turned toward Ruby. "But not you. You already got to go." It felt great, saying that to her. For once, he held the upper hand.

"What?" Ruby said, obviously infuriated. "I know I got to go once, but I really want to do it again! It's just so cool! I mean, it's living history! I love history. It's an amazing thing to study, and to actually get to go back and meet all of them is totally unreal!"

It was, Oliver knew. But . . . "Let me go up and get the hat and see what it thinks," he said, and he put the remains of his snack on the table and ran up the stairs.

He figured maybe he should wait for Sam to discuss the Ava and J.P. situation with the hat, but he certainly could ask it about his sisters. He picked it up and took it out of the bag, setting it down on his bed.

"So, my sisters," he began.

The hat burped gently and shifted around on the bed. "Sisters, yes," it murmured, seeming to still be half asleep. "Ah, yes, sisters." It paused for a moment. "Mr. Jefferson had several sisters. His favorite was named Jane. She played the harpsichord and encouraged Mr. Jefferson as a child to take up the violin, which he did."

Oliver had known that. "My favorite sister is Cassie," he said. "And she feels bad that she hasn't had a chance to travel back in time. But now Ruby, who's not my favorite sister, wants to have another adventure. And I really don't want her there. She just bosses me around and acts all critical of me. All the time! She just never stops!" He could tell he was getting upset. He should probably try to calm down a little.

"Take some deep breaths," the hat counseled, in its high, squeaky voice. "Breathe in, breathe out. Relax." It sounded sort of like one of his mom's yoga videos. "Deep breaths."

Oliver lay down on his bed, next to the hat, and breathed deeply, in and out, and soon he realized that he was feeling better.

"Thanks," he said. "That actually helped!"

"Of course it did," the hat said. "So what I would advise is that all three of you come on an adventure. Perhaps it will do wonders for your relationship. Let me come down and discuss this with all of you."

Oliver jumped up, put the hat on his head, and returned to the family room.

"So?" Ruby said. "We've been sitting and sitting. Waiting and waiting. What were you doing up there?"

"Well?" Cassie joined in. "You know, I haven't even heard the hat speak."

"Do you doubt me?" the hat said, an edge to its tone. Oliver took a deep breath, hoping the hat wouldn't go into one of its angry fits.

Cassie turned pale. "Wow," she said shakily. "You really do talk. No, I mean, I didn't exactly doubt you, but . . ."

"I do find that humans have a very limited view of the capacity of hats, as I was saying to Oliver recently," the hat continued. "It's a form of objectism, I would say. You humans have a real superiority complex. Little do you know what hats are capable of!"

"I'm sure you're right," Cassie said soothingly. "It's just that hats don't usually show us that they can do stuff like talking."

"You are a kind young lady," the hat said. "Very kind indeed."

Cassie smiled at the hat.

"I think the three of you need to go on an adventure together," the hat said, "as I was telling Oliver upstairs. But not today. I need to think about a good place and time for you three. Something that will be most meaningful and memorable. Perhaps tomorrow? Or over the weekend?"

Cassie and Ruby looked disappointed.

"Well, okay," they both said together.

"I'm going over to the park," Oliver said. He kind of wanted to get away from them.

"Take the iPad," Cassie said, handing it to him. "Put it in a backpack and bring it with you, okay? Text us that you got there. And check in from time to time so we know where you are."

"Where else would I be?" Oliver said. Honestly, the park was two blocks away. And there usually were other kids hanging out there. Cassie tended to be overprotective. "But if I had my own phone, that would certainly help."

And, with the hat still on his head, he headed out the door, bringing the basketball with him. As he approached the park—he did send Cassie a text indicating where he was—he could see a few kids over by the basketball court, and when he drew closer, he could see it was Sam, Andrew, Colin, and Rhiannon.

"Oliver!" Colin said. "You want to play?"

"Sure," Oliver said, and he joined in. But after a few minutes, someone emerged onto the front steps of Colin and Rhiannon's house and summoned them inside.

"Our babysitter," Rhiannon said. "See you guys later."

And Andrew said he should go too, because he had baseball practice.

Which left Sam and Oliver.

"Do you want to play basketball some more?" Oliver asked. "Or I thought maybe the hat . . ." This might be a good time for the hat to spring into action.

"The hat, definitely," Sam said. "I mean, if it wants to."

"Right," Oliver said, and before he knew it, his head felt like it was spinning, and then the two of them were sitting, dazed, on a grassy spot on a hillside. Oliver could see Monticello in the distance. Next to him and Sam was an older version of Thomas Jefferson, his face lined and his hair mostly white. He seemed very busy with a device of some kind, adjusting it and peering into it. A telescope? Oliver wasn't sure.

"What's that?" Oliver inquired. "A telescope? And what are you doing with it?"

"Oh, Oliver," Thomas Jefferson said, moving away

from the telescope and looking slightly startled. He looked down at them. "Yes, of course it is a telescope. I am planning to watch the upcoming eclipse and document it. And Sam, hello. I have not seen you in a while."

"Hello, sir," Sam said politely, standing up. Oliver did the same. "A solar eclipse?"

"Why, yes," Thomas Jefferson said. "I have long been interested in such phenomena. Did you know that I bought my first telescope back in 1786? In London? This particular telescope, however, I purchased in 1793."

"You're not supposed to look right at an eclipse," Oliver said. He remembered that from an eclipse that had happened recently, back in the twenty-first century. "Unless you have protective glasses, or whatever."

"They probably didn't have protective glasses in whatever year we're in," Sam hissed at Oliver.

"Oh, yeah," Oliver said.

"Protective glasses?" Thomas Jefferson said. "You are referring to smoked glass? For the telescope?"

"I guess so," Oliver said. "Yes." So they had put the protective glass on the telescope rather than on the person? Interesting.

"Ah, here they come now," Thomas Jefferson said, glancing toward Monticello. "I have the honor of welcoming my old and dear friend, President Madison, to view the eclipse with me, together with his secretary, Mr. Coles."

Two men were indeed approaching, a third shape hovering behind them. It was shimmering and bright.

"What's that?" Oliver said, gesturing at the shimmering shape.

"That, my dear Oliver, is the president of the United

States," Thomas Jefferson said, sounding a little reproachful. "The position I held before he assumed it. James Madison. And his secretary, as I have already mentioned."

"No, the thing next to them," Oliver said. "That shimmering thing."

"Yeah," Sam joined in. "I've seen something like that before, when I was with George . . . ," and he stopped.

George Washington? Maybe these early leaders of the country carried shimmering shapes around with them, Oliver thought. But then wouldn't someone have written about that before?

"I see no shimmering thing," Thomas Jefferson said. "Only people. Although I grow old, so perhaps my vision is not as good as it once was."

"What's today's date?" Oliver asked. "How old are you?" He wanted to know, so why not ask?

"Oliver, really," Thomas Jefferson said, sounding a little like Ruby. Or maybe the hat. "The date is September 17, 1811, and I am sixty-eight years old."

"Okay, thanks," Oliver said. The two men and the shimmering shape had drawn closer. Several chairs had been set out on the ground, and Thomas Jefferson, James Madison, and Edward Coles sat down. Edward Coles looked a lot younger than the other two.

"Mr. President," Thomas Jefferson said to James Madison. "May I present Oliver and Sam?"

"Yes, of course," James Madison said. "And my secretary, Mr. Coles."

They all nodded at one another. Wow, Oliver thought. Now he had met five of the first six presidents. He was just missing the fifth, James Monroe.

The shimmering shape had moved closer to James Madison, hovering near his chair. For whatever reason, Oliver suddenly thought of his table group at school. But why would a shimmering shape near Monticello in 1811 remind him of school, anyway? He tried to put it out of his head.

". . . when you were in Paris," James Madison was saying to Thomas Jefferson. "So many wonderful things you sent me. The pocket telescope. The pedometer. A Swiss watch." He had a nostalgic look in his eye.

"Yes, of course," Thomas Jefferson said, also seeming nostalgic. "And naturally you sent me many things in return. The fruit tree grafts. The pecans. The sugar maple seeds. But I recall that you were unable to send the live opossum that I requested."

And the two men burst into laughter, Edward Coles smiling too.

Meanwhile, the shimmering shape had come up to Oliver and Sam. It was moving what looked like its arms back and forth. This was making Oliver nervous. Sam looked kind of worried. The shape seemed to shrug a little, then back away.

The three men were apparently oblivious. They continued to talk, about the upcoming eclipse, about problems with Britain, about the political situation.

"This shimmering thing reminds me of something that happened when I was at George's swearing-in," Sam whispered to Oliver. "As president. There were these two shapes hovering around John Adams. And for some reason they reminded me . . ." And he paused. He looked

97

stunned. "Oh my god," he said. "I think I know what they were now. And this shape might be someone from our class. Somehow I'm getting the sense that it is. Someone who's made a connection to James Madison."

"I was thinking that too," Oliver whispered back. "I was thinking of my table group at school. So maybe it's one of those kids. But what were the two shapes?" Oh! Of course! "Ava and J.P.? But why couldn't you see them? And why can't we see this thing?"

The shape seemed to fold its arms and glare at them. As if it was angry.

"We need to talk to the hat," Oliver said. "Now." And he started to take it off his head, but then he thought of Sam, and how maybe Sam would want to stay back in 1811, so he put the hat back on. But something had gone wrong. They weren't outside anymore. They weren't back home either. They were in a room. Three men in old-fashioned garb were seated around a wooden table laden with food, eating and talking.

"What the . . ." Sam whispered. "What just happened?"

"I'm not sure," Oliver replied, trying to keep his voice down. He looked at the three men. One was definitely Thomas Jefferson, and another appeared to be James Madison. But they looked a lot younger than they had in 1811.

"I kind of wanted to see the eclipse," Sam said. "But maybe this is just as well. Maybe we would have ended up with some big eye problem because the protection wasn't good enough. Maybe . . . ," and his voice trailed off.

". . . location of the US capital," Thomas Jefferson

was saying.

"But the debt issue," the third man said. "Have we reached an accord?"

Oliver stared at the third man. He looked extremely familiar.

"Alexander Hamilton?" Sam hissed at him, gesturing toward the table.

Of course! The face pictured on all the ten-dollar bills. The first US Treasury secretary. The subject of the famous musical that a couple of kids in Ms. Martin's class had seen. And Thomas Jefferson's enemy. Oliver had devoted part of his report to their disagreements. Hamilton had favored more of a British-style approach for the new country, with a stronger central government, while Jefferson had been concerned that such thinking could lead back to monarchy.

"I thought they hated each other," Sam whispered. "Why are they eating together, anyway?"

Oliver tried to remember. Something about a compromise Thomas Jefferson had worked out. Locating the nation's capital in Washington, DC, in exchange for a deal on the role of the federal government in taking care of states' financial debts. He had invited Hamilton and Madison, who represented opposing points of view, to dinner to discuss the matter. Some time around 1790, from what Oliver recalled. Thomas Jefferson must have been secretary of state at the time. He whispered all of this to Sam, who nodded.

"You know, this happened to me once with George," Sam said. "I sort of took the hat off for a second, and all of a sudden I was a few months ahead. But I was still at Valley Forge. This is more, like, a huge jump back in time. And to a whole different place. I don't get it."

Oliver thought about this. He didn't get it either. And this definitely wasn't Monticello. Where did this dinner happen, anyway? Philadelphia, maybe? No, it had been New York City.

"Oliver, Sam," Thomas Jefferson suddenly said, fixing his eyes upon them. "So nice to see you. Won't you join us for dinner? James Hemings has prepared a feast! Capon! Meringues! Bell fritters!"

James Hemings? One of Madison Hemings's relatives, no doubt. Oliver had an idea of what meringues were, a kind of dessert, but capon and bell fritters? He was curious.

"Sure!" he said. He looked around the table at what appeared to be a mouth-watering display of food.

Sam nodded.

"Who have we here?" Alexander Hamilton asked, gazing in a puzzled way at Oliver and Sam. "Are you here to help negotiate away our troubles?"

"I think they are just here to observe," James Madison said. "Surely they are too young to serve as negotiators?"

"They are friends, gentlemen," Thomas Jefferson said. "Witnesses to what diplomacy can do to settle a vexing question." And he gave a half smile and looked around the table at the two other men and Oliver and Sam.

Oliver was about to help himself to some food, when Alexander Hamilton spoke. "Quite an impressive hat, young man," he said, turning toward Oliver. "May I take a look?"

Oh no. Not again. But he needed to be polite, so he

started to hand the hat over, and then he and Sam were back in the park. No sign of Jefferson, Hamilton, or Madison. Or the food. Well, at least this would give him the chance to interrogate the hat about the shimmering shape. And about how they jumped back in time from 1811 to 1790.

He could hear Sam sigh. "That food looked good," Sam said. "I kind of wanted to try it."

"So what's the deal?" Oliver said, taking the hat off and giving it a stern look. "Why can we see things sometimes and not other times? Who was that with James Madison in 1811, anyway? And how did we end up in 1790?"

"Yeah," Sam said, focusing back on the hat. "You really need to explain all of this. Now."

"Ah, well," the hat said. "The mysteries of time travel. Who can see things and who can't. It's all quite confusing, really. And the jumping back twenty-one years? I am not certain how that happened myself! I do quite amaze myself with my talents at times." It seemed quite pleased with itself, Oliver thought. "I am delighted that you made the acquaintance of Mr. Hamilton."

"But how come I couldn't see Ava and J.P. that time with George? And we couldn't see whoever this was with James Madison?" Sam asked, returning to the first topic at hand.

"And Ava and J.P. couldn't see me that time in Paris, but I could see them?" Oliver added.

"Yes, yes," the hat said. "I wouldn't delve too deeply into all of that if I were you. Just let certain things be."

"But . . . ," Sam began.

Oliver sighed. It was clear the hat didn't really understand the whole seeing-not-seeing issue. Still, he could certainly ask it about the bobblehead. "Why didn't Ava and J.P. have a hat?" he inquired. "Why did they have a John Adams bobblehead?"

"Perhaps that's a New England thing," the hat said. "Really, Oliver, I do not know. Now stop asking me all these questions! I must rest! I am very tired!"

Oliver put the hat back on his head, where he could feel the rumblings of the hat's snores. "I didn't even get to ask it another question I've been thinking about," he told Sam, as they left the park. "Should we discuss all of this with Ava and J.P.?"

"I've been wondering that too," Sam said. "But we probably should ask the hat first."

Back at home, Oliver was about to put the hat in his room when Cassie stuck her head out of her door and intercepted him.

"Jared and Arlo were trying to Facetime you," she said. "I told them you'd call them back once you were home."

Jarlo! That was good. Oliver realized he hadn't thought about them for a while. He put the hat back in its Mount Vernon bag and called them back.

"Hey, Oliver!" Jared said.

"Hi!" Arlo chimed in.

They were both cramming their faces into the screen, as they tended to do.

"So I found some kids here, who also are twins, who want to do the cow project for our science fair," Oliver announced.

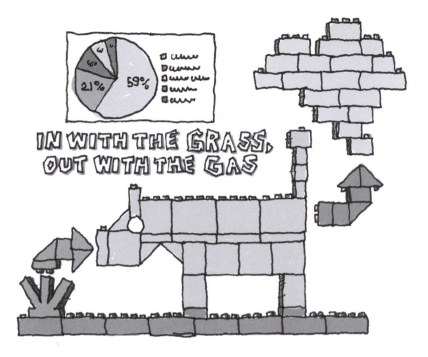

"Cool," Jared and Arlo said together.

"Maybe the six of us can Facetime and combine forces," Oliver continued. The idea had just come to him, but it sounded good. Even if Arun had to be part of the whole thing.

"Great!" Jared said, and he started discussing the diorama they were planning and the posters, and the issue of how to actually get the plastic cow in the diorama to emit anything at all, much less methane gas.

"Yes, that's definitely a problem," Oliver conceded. "Maybe the gas will just have to be imaginary. Or maybe it could be bubbles, like one of those bubble-blowing machines."

He wondered what Thomas Jefferson would do if he were asked to make a diorama of a cow emitting gas. Oliver was sure he'd come up with a creative solution based on the best eighteenth- or nineteenth-century science. He'd have to ask him the next time he saw him. He knew there had been cattle at Monticello, so he was sure Thomas Jefferson would be familiar with everything about them.

As Jarlo kept talking about the project, Oliver wondered if he should tell them about meeting Thomas Jefferson. About meeting Madison Hemings. He would have before, obviously. But . . .

"Oh, we have to get off," Jared suddenly announced. "Homework." And the twins' faces vanished from the screen.

Oliver realized he had homework too, and then there was dinner, and then he decided to read some more about cows, and then he read more about eclipses and telescopes, and by then it was time to go to sleep.

The next day at lunch, he filled Colin and Rhiannon in on some of what he had learned about cows.

Katie, who happened to be sitting near them, leaned over. "Hey, can I join in on your project?" she asked. "It sounds really fun. And I was going to work with Ava and Samantha, but they want to do something about cats because they both have cats, and I don't have a cat, so I'm not that interested. Not that I have a cow, either, but . . ."

Colin and Rhiannon looked at Oliver. As if he were the one who should be deciding.

"Yeah, sure," he said. "That would be good."

Katie smiled. "Great!" she said, sounding excited.

The four of them went out together for recess. Tom and Ryan stood on the field, preparing to choose the games and the teams.

"Soccer," Tom announced. "And I want Colin on my team."

Ryan looked around at the assorted boys, plus Katie and Rhiannon. "I'll take Sam," he said.

Everyone looked shocked, including Sam.

"What?" Tom said. "I mean, there's Andrew, and James, and Rhiannon, and . . ."

"I've decided," Ryan said.

"Your loss," Tom muttered, and quickly chose Andrew for his team.

Oliver was puzzled. Was Ryan actually being nice in some way? And why? He wondered if Sam understood what was going on. He should ask him later.

He was picked toward the end, for Ryan's team, and during the game found himself preoccupied with various questions. Would a bubble machine work for the cow project? Should he and Sam ask Ava about why she and J.P. were friends with the Adams family? Maybe he could borrow the John Adams bobblehead and go on an adventure with it himself! But would that work? Maybe the hat would get offended. And who was it that was traveling around with James Madison? Maybe . . .

"Oliver!" he heard, and suddenly the ball ricocheted off his foot and into the goal, past the diving

Andrew! What had just happened?

Everyone on his team started cheering. He apparently had just scored a goal, completely by accident. He hadn't even been paying attention. Not only that, it was the game-winning goal, because the score had been tied at 2–2, and the recess monitors were blowing the whistles for everyone to go inside.

"Great goal, Oliver!" James said, giving him a high-five.

"That was really good," Andrew said, also high-fiving him. "I just couldn't get to it."

Oliver had scored goals before, but never the game winner. He could somehow hear the hat, back in its bag in his room, cheering too.

Chapter

~7~

All weekend, Cassie and Ruby kept bothering him about the hat. Why wasn't it doing anything? Hadn't it promised to take them somewhere? What was going on? Had it lost its magic powers?

This last question was something Oliver found himself getting increasingly worried about. He kept leaning over the Mount Vernon gift bag and once or twice resorted to giving the hat a gentle nudge, but nothing happened at all. It just kept snoring.

So he went to Tae Kwon Do both days, and he organized some ideas for the science fair project, and he spent some time at the park playing basketball with the other kids, and he managed to forget about the hat. At least every so often.

On Monday, toward the end of the school day, Ms. Martin wrote "The Bill of Rights" on the whiteboard. "Can anyone explain what that is?" she asked.

"The first ten amendments to the Constitution," Oliver said immediately. Oh, no. He should have raised his hand.

"Raise your hand, please, Oliver," Ms. Martin said.

"But yes, you're right. Can anyone name some of them?"

Rhiannon's hand immediately went up. "Freedom of speech," she said, once Ms. Martin had called on her. "Freedom of religion. Those are both part of the first amendment."

Oliver raised his hand. "Freedom of the press," he added. "That's also part of the first amendment. Did you know that Thomas Jefferson once wrote, 'Were it left to me to decide whether we should have a government without newspapers, or newspapers without a government, I should not hesitate a moment to prefer the latter'?" It was one of his favorite Thomas Jefferson quotes. Ruby had first told him about it. She liked it too, because it was pro-newspaper.

"Very good, Oliver, and Rhiannon too," Ms. Martin said.

"The brainiacs strike again," Tom whispered, loudly enough so everyone could hear him. A couple of kids laughed.

"Uncool," Colin said, glancing at Tom.

"I know they are," Tom shot back.

"No, you," Colin said. "Not them."

Everyone started talking at once, and Ms. Martin quickly clapped her hands five times to regain order.

Almost everyone clapped back, and then silence fell over the room.

"Tom, do you want to go to the office?" Ms. Martin said, frowning at him. "One more thing, and . . ."

"No," Tom said, looking really angry. He glared at Colin.

Oliver, for his part, sent Colin a grateful sort of look,

and Colin shook his head, as if to say, "No big deal." But it was a big deal, Oliver reflected. No one had ever stuck up for him like that. Not even Jarlo. Of course, Colin was probably mostly sticking up for his sister, but still.

As everyone packed up to leave for the day, Oliver realized he couldn't find his math worksheet, and he ended up being the last kid left in the classroom.

"Oliver, you're doing a fantastic job as Eastview Ambassador," Ms. Martin said, handing him an extra copy of the worksheet. "I think Colin and Rhiannon are settling in really well, and a lot of that is thanks to you." And she smiled at him.

Oliver smiled back at her. "Thanks," he said, as he dashed out the door to avoid missing the bus. But did Colin and Rhiannon's settling in really have anything to do with him? Somehow he sensed that Colin and Rhiannon were probably really good at settling in, whether or not they had an Eastview Ambassador helping them out.

He was still thinking about that when he got home and found Celia there. "I'm going to take you to Tae Kwon Do a little later, but do you have homework?" she inquired.

Oliver nodded. "But I just have to check something upstairs first," he said, running up to his room. Would the hat finally be awake?

He leaned over the bag.

"Aha!" the hat said, seeming energetic once more. "Oliver, my good friend!"

Oliver sighed with relief. He had been worried. "What happened to you over the weekend?" he asked it. "My sisters were all upset because you told them you'd take the three of us somewhere this weekend and you didn't."

"What?" the hat said. "But surely it is the weekend now!"

"No," Oliver said. "You slept through the whole weekend. It's Monday."

The hat looked appalled, if a hat can look that way. "Apologies, apologies," it said, seeming to shake its head. "How very embarrassing. Oh dear. I must tell your sisters how very sorry I am."

Oliver explained that his sisters weren't home, but that maybe it could take him on an adventure. Right now.

"And is anyone else home?" the hat inquired.

"Celia. She's sort of my babysitter. But maybe she won't notice if I'm gone for just a little while," Oliver said.

"Very well," the hat said. "I can arrange that."

Oliver put the hat on, and the dizzy feeling came over him, and he opened his eyes to find himself standing near Monticello. As usual, there were people bustling here and there, up and down what he realized was Mulberry Row. The row of cabins and buildings hummed with activity. Virtually all of these people, he knew, as he looked around at them, were enslaved. And there was Madison Hemings, approaching him.

"Hello," Madison Hemings said. He looked a little older. Maybe about Ruby's age. "It has been a while, has it not? Would you like to see the joiner's shop? I have been apprenticed to my uncle, as I believe I mentioned to you would happen."

Oliver stepped inside a large room, where several men

were busy fashioning wood into tables and chairs.

Madison Hemings led him over to one particular work in progress. It looked like it was going to become a chair. "You see?" he said. "My uncle has let me work on this piece alone. I used to merely carry things around for him, his tools and other necessities. But now he says I am old enough to try my own hand at carpentry."

Oliver peered at Madison Hemings's work. The wood looked smooth. Oliver ran his hand over what seemed like the back of the chair. He wondered what it would be like to be a fourteen-year-old carpenter's apprentice who could learn to read only from Thomas Jefferson's grandchildren. Even though he was Thomas Jefferson's son. And however bad Madison Hemings had it, Madison Hemings's life was no doubt better than that of other enslaved kids at Monticello. Oliver shook his head.

"We make furniture from various woods," Madison Hemings was saying. "Mahogany, walnut, cherry. I would introduce you to my uncle, but he has gone on an errand." He paused. "I keep asking you about your hat," he said. "And every time I do, you seem to disappear. It is quite strange."

Oliver sighed. He couldn't very well explain the whole thing to Madison Hemings, could he? But it would seem rude not to hand it over. Maybe for once the hat would suspend the rules? He thought about it for a minute and finally took the hat off, preparing to give it to Madison Hemings. And of course the hat did not suspend any rules. A second later, Madison Hemings, his handmade chair, and the whole joiner's shop were nowhere to be seen, and Oliver could hear Celia calling.

And a minute later, he heard a tapping at his bedroom door. "Oliver?"

He put the hat, which was grumbling something about how Oliver should have remembered the rules, back on his head and opened the door.

"I've been calling and calling!" Celia exclaimed, looking worried. "It's time to go to Tae Kwon Do! And what's your homework situation? Your mom mentioned that you haven't practiced the piano for more than a week, so you really should practice."

That was true; he hadn't. But no one had reminded him to, so it wasn't really his fault. He wasn't very good at the piano, anyway. He wanted to start on a different instrument, but he hadn't done anything about it yet. Maybe in middle school. He thought maybe he should try a more unusual instrument. The bass clarinet. The piccolo. The euphonium. The bassoon.

Celia propelled him and his Tae Kwon Do bag out the door, and on the way to the studio, his mind switched from music to science, and he started telling her about the science fair project. He thought maybe the bubbles would work for the gas, and Celia seemed to agree, and then she dropped him off and said she was running a few errands and would be back to pick him up.

In class, they were working on sparring, and he was paired with Katie, and even though Oliver was a five-striper and Katie only a one-striper, she was probably better at the various kicks and punches and blocks than he was. Was there anything he was actually good at? He wasn't sure.

"So are you ready for your black-belt exam?" Katie asked him at the end of class. "I just can't wait till I get to that point. But it's going to be a while."

Oliver nodded. "Well, maybe not totally ready, but I'm working on it."

"What did you think about the whole thing in class today?" she inquired. "With Tom and Colin?" Without waiting for an answer, she continued. "I've never seen anyone burn Tom like that. He really has it coming, you know? I heard Ryan's getting kind of tired of hanging out with Tom all the time. Did you hear that?"

Of course Oliver hadn't heard that. He hardly ever knew what was going on.

"You know Sophia C.?" Katie said. "The one in our class, not Sophia R. or Sophia N.?"

Oliver thought so. There were a lot of girls named Sophia. He couldn't keep all of them straight.

"So she really likes Tom. At least she used to. But now I heard she really likes Colin instead."

This was all completely beyond Oliver. How did she know all of this?

"Anyway, gotta go!" Katie said. "See you!" And she ran down the stairs.

Oliver followed, more slowly. He wondered again about what Ruby had said about their family's social skills. "So I took what was left over," she had said. "And poor Olls, well . . ." She had a point. No matter how encouraging Cassie had been the other day. It was clear that he, Oliver, had no social skills.

Celia was waiting outside. She waved her phone at him. "Nigel just texted me," she said. "Sam wanted to know if you guys could hang out once you were done with class. I said I'd have to double-check on your homework situation."

"I only have some reading, but that won't take too long. I can do it tonight," Oliver said. "Yeah, that would be good."

Celia suggested that both of them should go to Sam's house. "Nigel and I can study for our midterms," she said.

Oliver wondered why Sam wanted to get together. Did he really want to hang out, or did this have to do with the hat? Hadn't the hat said that Oliver could borrow it for a week or so? And it had been more than a week. Did that mean his adventures would be coming to an end soon? He started thinking about that, and by the time they had arrived at Sam's house, he was in a panic. His stomach was hurting. But he tried to do what the hat had told him. Take deep breaths. In and out. And once again, the deep breaths seemed to calm him down.

Both Sam and Nigel appeared at the door to meet them. Nigel immediately escorted Celia off to the family room, and Sam took Oliver up to his room.

"I'm still not sure what's going on with the two of

them," Sam said. "Whether she's actually his girlfriend or not."

"Ah, yes," the hat said suddenly. "I thought you told me she was soon to be his girlfriend. Didn't you?"

"I said I didn't know!" Sam said. "I just said he wanted her to be his girlfriend! You were the one who assumed it was about to happen!"

"I never did!" the hat said. "You did!"

"Stop arguing!" Oliver said. "You sound like me and Ruby!"

"Oh, dear," the hat said, and fell silent.

"We were wondering," Oliver said, figuring this was as good a time as any, "whether to ask Ava and J.P. about their time-travel adventures."

Sam nodded.

"Yes, yes," the hat said. "I have been thinking about that too. If the time is right, then discuss. If not, move along."

What? Oliver didn't understand.

But then he felt the room spin around, and suddenly he was in what looked like a really fancy old-fashioned office or library of some kind. Thomas Jefferson was sitting at a desk, which was strewn about with papers. He seemed to be deep in contemplation, reading whatever the papers contained. Oliver could see a fireplace along one wall, and a revolving bookstand that Thomas Jefferson probably had designed.

Oliver glanced at Sam, who was next to him. Where were they? Thomas Jefferson looked older than he had in Paris, but younger than the time when he was preparing to watch the eclipse. Maybe he was the president? Maybe this was the White House?

A knock sounded at the door. "Mr. President?" A young man stepped into the room. "Secretary Madison is here to see you. To discuss the Louisiana situation."

"Very well, send him in," Thomas Jefferson said, not looking up from his reading.

So he was the president! But what was the Louisiana situation? Could it be the Louisiana Purchase? Oliver thought back. He knew that during Thomas Jefferson's presidency, in 1803, the United States had bought a huge area of land, many states' worth, including Louisiana, from France. Was that what they were going to talk about?

"News from James Monroe in Paris," James Madison said, bustling into the room and proceeding over to Thomas Jefferson's desk. Oliver hadn't been focusing too much on James Madison the first time, but he noticed now that he was pretty short. Maybe only six inches taller than Oliver himself. Clearly way shorter than Thomas Jefferson. "Oh, I see you have visitors."

"Do I?" Thomas Jefferson said, looking up. "Why, yes, I do. Hello, Oliver and Sam. I did not know you were there. Oliver, Sam, Secretary of State Madison."

Oliver was about to point out that they had met James Madison before, but then he stopped. That had been at a later point in history. This was 1803, and that had been 1811. It would only confuse them.

So he just nodded, as did Sam, who seemed to be thinking along the same lines.

James Madison nodded back, before returning his attention to Thomas Jefferson.

"Negotiations are proceeding well, and Mr. Monroe and Mr. Livingston believe they are on the verge of an agreement," James Madison said, looking excited. "Just think of it, more than 800,000 square miles of new land belonging to our country! At a cost of $15 million!"

"Hmmm," Thomas Jefferson said, looking thoughtful. "Yes, and I have authorized that expedition to look into the territory and, I hope, far beyond. Well, good, good. It's certainly better than having Napoleon right there next to us."

Oliver was a little confused. "What exactly is the agreement about?" he inquired. "Is this the Louisiana Purchase? And what expedition? And is Napoleon in charge of France right now?"

Sam nodded, as if to join in on the question. He looked even more confused than Oliver felt.

Thomas Jefferson launched into an explanation. James Monroe and Robert Livingston were the envoys to France and were negotiating with the French government over a large piece of land that had belonged to Spain but now was coming under French control. Apparently the French, led by Napoleon, were not eager to control it, Thomas Jefferson said, so the United States was on the verge of becoming much larger.

"And the expedition," he added. "I think we shall have

some able men leading it. They are to traverse the new lands and, I hope, continue much farther. I have long been interested in exploring the West."

Was this the Lewis and Clark expedition that eventually reached the Pacific Ocean? Oliver wondered. He hadn't realized Thomas Jefferson had been behind it. But that made sense. Thomas Jefferson seemed consumed with curiosity about many things.

"Meriwether Lewis and William Clark are good men," Thomas Jefferson continued, as if reading Oliver's mind. "They should do well. I am eager to learn what they shall find."

Cool! Oliver wondered if maybe he could get the hat to take him along on the expedition.

"How old do you have to be to join the expedition?" Sam was asking.

"They probably could use some helpful boys," James Madison said, nodding at the two of them. "Perhaps we could have a word with them and see. But your families . . ."

"Yes," Thomas Jefferson broke in. "Would they agree?"

Well, of course not. But maybe they wouldn't have to know. Oliver and Sam exchanged glances. What would the hat say? Oliver pulled the hat off his head to ask it, and then found himself back in Sam's room. With Sam, but naturally without Thomas Jefferson and James Madison. And without a chance to join the expedition.

"Dang," Oliver said.

"I know," Sam said. "You're not so great at remembering to keep the hat on your head. Maybe we could have gone on the Lewis and Clark expedition! Maybe we could have been the youngest full-fledged explorers on the trip! Maybe . . . ," and his voice trailed off. He seemed to be imagining what could have been.

"Sorry," Oliver said. He felt kind of bad.

"It's okay," Sam said, snapping out of it. "I always forget too."

"Neither of you," the hat said, "is particularly mindful of the rules." It paused for a minute. "Ah, well," it continued. "Be that as it may, Oliver, I have come up with a plan for you and your sisters. It shall happen tonight."

"Can I come along?" Sam inquired.

"Perhaps," the hat said. "Depending on your respective families' schedules."

"Let's go downstairs," Oliver said. "Maybe we should head over to my house, then."

They clattered down the stairs, the hat back on Oliver's head, and rushed into the family room. Nigel and Celia were in the adjoining kitchen—Sam's house was very much like his own, Oliver noticed—sitting at the table drinking coffee.

"Yes, yes," the hat said loudly. "How are things between the two of you? I have been wondering."

Celia looked startled. "It really does talk," she said. "Wow." She looked back and forth between the hat and Nigel. "I wasn't sure whether to believe you."

"Of course I talk, young lady!" the hat said, sounding outraged. "Do you think hats can't talk? My question wasn't about my ability to speak; it was about how things are going between you two."

Nigel glared at Sam and Oliver and the hat. "Things

are going fine," he said. He gave Sam another look, and Sam pulled Oliver—and the hat—back toward the front door.

"Why'd you have to start in with that again?" Sam whispered to the hat. "Nigel's going to be really mad at me."

"Curiosity," the hat said. "Curiosity may have killed the cat, but not the hat. Although I do hope it didn't kill the cat. I'm quite fond of cats, really. One of my favorite books is *The Cat in the Hat*."

Oliver was somewhat amazed. Did the hat really read? It had indicated as much the other day, but . . .

"We're going over to Oliver's house," Sam called to Nigel and Celia.

"No you're not," Nigel called back. "At least, Sam, you're not. Remember the dinner for your dad's birthday?"

Sam slapped his forehead with his palm. "Oh, yeah," he said. "Well, good luck on the adventure with your sisters."

"Thanks," Oliver said. "I'm sorry you can't come along."

Celia emerged from the kitchen, Nigel following, and she and Oliver headed back toward his house. Both his sisters were home, so Celia said goodbye to everyone and departed.

"So here are we, the happy siblings three," the hat announced, as they all gathered in the family room. "I have figured out our plan."

"Will we be back in time for dinner?" Cassie said, looking worried. "I was supposed to get dinner started because our parents have to go to some work party and they won't be home till late."

"Dinner?" the hat said. "Well, you see, food is not an issue for hats, so I had not thought of that. Let us wait until after dinner, then. Oliver, please put me back in my bag so I can rest. I am very tired."

Oliver did so. He could barely make it through dinner, and then he realized he hadn't done his homework, so he finished that in record time, and then he took the hat out of the bag.

"Ready?" he asked.

"If your sisters are," it replied, seeming perky and awake.

Oliver put the hat on and knocked on each sister's door in turn. Cassie emerged, looking excited. Ruby peered out, seeming to be in a bad mood.

"This French homework is driving me crazy," she said. "But let's go! I'll just have to finish up later. So where exactly are we going?"

The hat coughed self-importantly before speaking. "I assume you know that Mr. Jefferson served as governor of Virginia during the Revolutionary War. And the British were threatening the state throughout his term. And in June of 1781, they attacked. Mr. Jefferson sent his family to what he hoped was a safe place while he was in danger. They sought to capture him."

Oliver had known this. Cassie and Ruby nodded.

"It was a most perilous time," the hat continued. "I would advise that the three of you stay close together. Be alert. Always look around you with care. And look after one another."

Cassie nodded again, while Oliver saw Ruby give him

a glance, as if to say, yeah, right. He wondered if, in a time of peril, Ruby would look after him. Would he look after her? Well, it probably wouldn't come to that.

Oliver blinked a few times and felt the dizzy feeling come over him, and he heard lots of screaming and yelling—he figured it must be Cassie, because Ruby had already experienced the whole thing before—and when he opened his eyes he was outside Monticello. It seemed smaller than its present-day version, and smaller than how it had looked at the time of the eclipse.

Various people were rushing around outside the grounds, and a large horse-drawn carriage was pulling up outside the house.

"They really are coming this time," one man cried to another as they passed each other. "The British!"

The horses whinnied, and one of the men driving the carriage leaped down, tossing the reins to the other. "I shall go find them now," he said, and dashed through the door into the house.

Oliver turned his attention from the men and the horses to Cassie and Ruby. Cassie was clutching onto Ruby's arm, staring around at her surroundings, her mouth open in what looked like complete shock.

Ruby, meanwhile, had her phone out, ready to record. "Testing, testing," she said. "I'm here at Monticello in what must be the late spring of 1781. Monticello is preparing for an invasion from British troops. I am interested in learning not just about Thomas Jefferson's role, but about what women experienced during this crucial time. What exactly was the role of women during the Revolutionary period? Testing. Testing." And she tried to play back what she had recorded. But nothing happened. "What the . . . ," she said, glaring at Oliver. "Why isn't my phone working?"

"Did they have phones in the eighteenth century?" Oliver shot back. Jeez. Why would she think her cell phone would work in the year 1781, anyway?

Ruby gave him a triumphant look. "Well, fortunately I have a reporter's notebook and a pen," she said, pulling the notebook from her pocket and the pen out from behind her ear. And she started scribbling away.

Oliver sighed. It would have been amazing if she had been unprepared, but no such luck.

"So, Ollie," Cassie said, her voice shaking a little. "What do we do next?"

"Normally, either Thomas Jefferson or Madison Hemings will show up," Oliver said. "Although Madison Hemings wasn't born yet at this point, so it's likely to be Thomas Jefferson."

And a minute later, sure enough, there he was, surrounded by a group of men and one woman and two girls. One girl looked like she was maybe three, and the other was probably a little younger than Oliver.

"I will come to you soon," Thomas Jefferson said, embracing the woman and the two girls. The younger one clung to him, while the older one squared her shoulders and climbed up into the carriage. "Polly, you be a good girl and listen to Patsy and to your mamma." And as the woman also sat down in the carriage, joining the older girl, he handed the younger one over. A moment later, amid various fits of hand-waving and calls of farewell, the carriage pulled out, leaving dust in its wake.

"Oh my god," Cassie was saying. She was gazing at the retreating shape of the carriage as it grew smaller and smaller. "So that's Thomas Jefferson? And his wife and his daughters? Unbelievable."

Thomas Jefferson was consulting with the group of men who surrounded him. Who were they, Oliver wondered.

"You have breakfasted well?" Thomas Jefferson was saying.

In the midst of a possible invasion, Thomas Jefferson was offering breakfast to these men? That seemed crazy. But people did need to eat. He wondered what the breakfast had been. Was there any more? He did feel a little hungry. And kind of hot. The hat felt wet and drippy on his head. But he knew better than to remove it.

"Absolutely, yes," one man was saying. They all seemed to be preparing to leave. As they mounted their horses and climbed into their carriages, Oliver looked around. Cassie was standing next to him, but Ruby—together with her pen and notebook—seemed to have vanished.

"Hey, where's Ruby?" Oliver said, poking Cassie in the arm.

"What?" Cassie said. She still seemed in a trance. "Ruby? She was just here, wasn't she?" She glanced toward Thomas Jefferson, who was rapidly heading back into the house. "Do you think she went inside?"

"Well, she could have," Oliver said. "I mean, no one would have stopped her, given everything that was going on, you know?"

Cassie sighed. "Let's look, then," she said, sounding more like herself.

So the two of them hurried into Monticello. It looked different from what Oliver had seen on the tour. He knew the house had been renovated many times, so that made sense. But honestly, he didn't really have a chance to look at the house. Cassie was dragging him rapidly through all the rooms, calling out Ruby's name over and over. Their voices echoed. The place seemed empty.

There was no sign of Ruby anywhere. Oliver felt a prickle of fear run through him. Where could she be?

Chapter
~8~

They started looking outside, running through the gardens and down various pathways. No one seemed to be around to ask if they had seen her.

"Oh no," Cassie said, as the two of them returned to the front of the house. She looked completely panic-stricken and out of breath. And really sweaty. Oliver assumed he did too. "Where on earth could she have gone? And in the middle of an invasion too!"

Oliver sat down on the grass to think. What had Ruby said when she was recording that useless thing into her useless phone? Maybe there was some clue there. Hadn't she said something about not just focusing on Thomas Jefferson but on women? Aha!

"The carriage!" he announced.

"The carriage?" Cassie repeated. Her eyes grew wide. "Yeah, the carriage! Ollie, you're such a genius! Focusing on the role of women! That's right!"

Ruby must have snuck into the carriage with Mrs. Jefferson and the girls while no one was looking. But where was the carriage going? And would she be safe on the road if the British really were on their way? He was sure Ruby must be getting some good information for whatever this project of hers was, from Mrs. Jefferson and probably the older girl too. But it seemed kind of risky. And now she was off somewhere without the protection of the hat. Which, he knew from his own experience a few weeks earlier, was not a good idea.

"Oh, Ollie," Cassie said, sitting down next to him and sighing again. "The hat said the three of us should stick together. And I should have kept a better eye on Ruby. I'm the oldest. I should have been more responsible." She took Oliver's hand and clutched it. "You're not leaving my side, okay?"

"Yeah," Oliver said. Jeez. She was holding his hand so hard it was starting to annoy him. He tried to pull his hand away. "I'm sure we'll find her." He wasn't so sure, but he thought if he was optimistic, maybe it would cheer Cassie up.

"Thanks, Ollie," Cassie said. She gave him a half-hearted smile. "But maybe we should go find Thomas Jefferson. Ask him where Ruby might be."

That was a good idea. Thomas Jefferson probably would know, being something of a genius himself.

"Maybe the hat knows where she is," Cassie added, as they got up. She brushed some pieces of grass and dirt off her jeans. "Oh, hat?"

Oliver shook his head. "It doesn't talk when we're on these trips. I'm not sure why."

Cassie shrugged. "Who knows," she said. "But would it talk if we went back home?"

Oliver was shocked. "We can't do that!" he said. "What

if it doesn't let us get back, and Ruby's trapped here forever?" He thought about that idea again. Maybe it wouldn't be so bad, actually. Maybe Ruby wouldn't mind. Maybe it would be kind of cool being in a different century from her for a while. He pondered some more. But forever? Well . . .

"Why wouldn't the hat let us come right back here if we went home for a minute?" Cassie said, seeming confused. "I don't understand."

Oliver explained that the hat had told Sam to lend it to Oliver for about a week, and it had been more than a week, so he wasn't sure what the situation was. And what if it suddenly decided that it was tired, or that it wanted to go back to Sam immediately, or that it just didn't want to take them back there to that particular year again? It was very grouchy sometimes.

"Oh," Cassie said, nodding. "That makes sense now. Well, why don't we go back inside Monticello and find Thomas Jefferson, then. This is urgent. We really need to locate Ruby, as soon as possible. Mom and Dad will kill me if we don't." And she marched briskly into the house.

Oliver followed her. They didn't have to go far. Thomas Jefferson was right there, in the front hallway. He seemed to be in a big hurry. He was holding something that sort of resembled the telescope he had been using during the eclipse.

"Oh, Oliver," he said, appearing slightly stressed out. "You have caught me at a bad time, I'm afraid. The British are approaching, and I have heard they are specifically searching for me. Mrs. Jefferson and the children have gone to what we hope is a safe location." He looked around. "I have been trying to move my papers so they will not be discovered. And Martin Hemings is trying to hide the silver."

Martin Hemings. Oliver assumed this was yet another of Madison Hemings's relatives on his mom's side. Oliver would have to google Martin Hemings once he got home.

"My sister is missing," Oliver said. That was the important thing, not Thomas Jefferson's silver. "We need you to help us."

"Is this not your sister?" Thomas Jefferson said, turning his attention briefly toward Cassie. "I recall meeting you a long time ago."

Cassie wasn't saying anything. She seemed momentarily tongue-tied at the thought of actually talking to Thomas Jefferson.

Oliver had no such qualms. "My other sister," he said. "Ruby. This isn't Ruby at all. This is Cassie." Oliver looked at Cassie more closely. She did resemble Ruby, now that he thought about it. And himself, too, except that he was a boy and they weren't.

"My apologies," Thomas Jefferson said graciously. "You all do have a certain family resemblance."

"She's in the carriage," Oliver blurted out. "At least, we think she's in the carriage."

Thomas Jefferson looked puzzled. "The carriage?" he said.

"With Mrs. Jefferson and your daughters," said Cassie, apparently regaining her powers of speech. "We believe she somehow got in there because she wanted to talk to them about the role of women in the Revolutionary

War, or something like that."

"The role of women," Thomas Jefferson repeated. "Interesting. What might the role of women be?"

"Like, why weren't women in the Declaration of Independence?" Cassie said. "And furthermore, why didn't you do anything about slavery? Why did life, liberty, and the pursuit of happiness apply only to white men?"

"Yeah," Oliver said, giving Cassie a mental high-five that he hoped she somehow received.

"I would love to discuss the role of women with you at greater length, but this is not the time," Thomas Jefferson said. "As I have told you, the British are looking for me. I should like to observe from a nearby hill to see what I can find. You see, I have my spyglass with me." And he gestured at the object in his hand. "I hope to talk with you further about this worthwhile topic at a better time." And he strode out of the house.

"Well, that wasn't very helpful," Oliver said. "Maybe you're right. Maybe we should go back home and see if the hat can tell us anything." And before he could think about it anymore, he grabbed Cassie's hand and took off the hat.

And there they were, back in the upstairs hallway outside Cassie's bedroom. They did a quick search of their house, just in case Ruby might have somehow spirited herself back to the twenty-first century. But there was no sign of her. Just as they had returned to the upstairs hallway, Oliver heard a key turning in the front door's lock.

"Do you think that's Ruby?" he said, preparing to run down the stairs.

"Kids?" It was his dad's voice at the front door. Oh no. Weren't they supposed to be at some office dinner or something? How late was it, anyway? "How's the homework coming along? The dinner ended earlier than we thought, so here we are!"

His dad peered up the staircase at Oliver and Cassie. "Hey, Ollie. Cassie. Where's Ruby?"

Oliver looked at Cassie, in a panic. What should they say? Your middle child is stuck in the eighteenth century during the British invasion of Virginia? We think she's with Thomas Jefferson's family? Obviously they couldn't say anything like that, could they?

"At a friend's house, doing homework," Cassie said quickly.

Oliver's mom appeared next to his dad. She closed the front door behind her. "It's getting kind of late," she said. "I'll text her and tell her I'll pick her up now. Which friend was it?"

Cassie mumbled something. She was fidgeting around, twisting her hands together, which Oliver knew meant she was nervous.

"What, sweetheart?" their mom said. "I couldn't hear you."

"I'll text her myself," Cassie said. "It's a girl in her history class. You don't know her. But she's really nice. Ruby said she'd need to stay there a little late because it's a big project that's due tomorrow."

Wow. Cassie was a good liar, Oliver thought. He hadn't realized how talented she was at inventing things on the spot. Maybe it was part of her acting abilities.

"Okay," his mom said. "Just tell her we'll pick her up at nine-thirty at the latest."

"Sure thing," Cassie said, and she pulled Oliver into her room and closed the door.

"Good job," Oliver said.

Cassie let out a deep breath and twisted her hands around some more. "All we need is to have Mom and Dad texting Ruby, and obviously she wouldn't answer. And what is she doing back there, and is she going to be okay?" Her voice was kind of shaky. As if she might cry. "I mean, she's in the middle of a war, you know?"

"Young lady, your sister is indeed back there, and I will take both of you back if you would like," the hat said suddenly.

Oliver felt a wave of relief hit him. Cassie grabbed the hat and hugged it. "Oh, thank you! Thank you!" she exclaimed. "Can you take us back right now? Can you make it so our parents don't remember any of this?"

"Your parents are not going to be an issue," the hat said. "But let us focus on finding Ruby, shall we?" And it seemed to nod at Oliver.

He replaced the hat on his head and took Cassie's hand again, and suddenly they were back outside Monticello. He let her hand go.

"But this isn't where Ruby is!" Cassie said, her voice getting shaky again. "What are we doing here, anyway? Where is she?"

Oliver felt panicky himself. What would they do if they never found her? And what if she really hadn't been in the carriage with the Jeffersons at all? What if she had been captured by the British? And what if she tried to interview them and was thrown into some horrible eighteenth-century jail?

"I shall need Caractacus," he heard, and Thomas Jefferson appeared from around the corner. He was out of breath. "The British!" he said. "I spied them with my spyglass from the top of Carters Mountain. I must ride away now to join my family! Shall I find horses for you so you can also escape? I believe the British will be here in just a few minutes."

Oliver wasn't sure what to say. He was actually kind of scared of horses. He remembered going on a pony ride when he was really little and crying a lot, and Ruby making fun of him. Some things never changed.

"Yes," Cassie said. "Thank you. Ollie can ride with me." Oh, that's right. She had taken riding lessons for years back in New Jersey. But she had stopped a while ago.

Thomas Jefferson was running off in another direction. They followed him.

"Do you still remember how?" Oliver asked Cassie. "To ride?" His stomach was starting to hurt. This wasn't good. He remembered the deep breathing exercise the hat had taught him, and tried to take a few deep breaths. In and out.

"Of course," Cassie said. "I know this isn't your favorite mode of transportation, but we're back in the eighteenth century, Ollie. Like, no cars. So this is pretty much the only way to see if Ruby actually is with the Jeffersons. And it's the only way to escape from the British. We're going to have to follow him."

A few minutes later, they were galloping off after Thomas Jefferson. Oliver was clutching on to Cassie for dear life. It was impossible to take any deep breaths. He was way too nervous. He was looking back and forth to see if he could spot a British soldier hiding off the pathway. But as they got farther and farther from Monticello, he still hadn't seen any. And soon it became clear that this was going to be a long ride.

Thomas Jefferson kept going, and his horse must have been stronger and faster than their horse, because the distance between them grew. Was its name really Caractacus? Oliver would have to check that once they got home. If they ever did. And it wasn't possible to talk to Cassie because they were moving so fast and she couldn't hear what he was saying even when he screamed at her. What if they got there and Ruby wasn't there? What then?

"What if she's not there?" he tried shouting to Cassie for what seemed like the millionth time. It never hurt to try again. But she didn't hear him. The wind blew into his face, and he held on tighter to Cassie. He wondered what would happen if Ruby had just magically disappeared into the past. Would she end up living in eighteenth- and then nineteenth-century Virginia? Would she perhaps become a pioneering woman journalist? Were there even women journalists back then? What would become of her? What would their family be like if she were trapped back in time and couldn't get out?

The horse seemed to be slowing down, and far ahead he could make out a house and a tiny figure dismounting from another horse. It must be Thomas Jefferson, he thought.

"Where are we?" he asked. Maybe Cassie could hear him now.

"What?" she called back. "Are you okay, Ollie?"

"Yes," he shouted back. The horse was moving really slowly now, and they were coming closer and closer to the house. He found that his stomach was feeling a little better at the prospect of getting off the horse.

He could see Mrs. Jefferson and the younger girl running out of the house, and the three of them hugging one another. But where was Ruby? And where was the older girl? Thomas Jefferson started pacing around. He looked upset, as did Mrs. Jefferson. The little girl was crying. Oh no.

"Oh my god," Cassie was saying. "Oh my god. Where is she? Why do they look so upset? What happened?"

She pulled the horse up next to the Jeffersons, and it neighed loudly. "Hello, excuse me, Governor, Mrs. Jefferson; have you seen our sister?" she inquired.

Oliver wasn't sure how to get off the horse. He felt sort of ridiculous. "Ruby," he contributed. "She's missing."

"Yes, and so is Patsy!" Mrs. Jefferson said, looking pale. "They went out for a walk, hours ago now, and they never came back. And I do not know if the British are aware of where we are, but I fear they may have captured both girls!"

"Oh, no," he heard Cassie sigh. "At least we know she was here, so that's something. But where could they have gone?"

The younger girl, Polly, was sniffling and whimpering. "I want Patsy!" she cried. "And our new friend. I quite liked her!"

Oliver was always surprised when people liked Ruby. But then again, she was nicer to most people than she was to him. And she was missing, so he probably shouldn't be thinking bad things about her now. Right?

"I shall go search for them," Thomas Jefferson said, getting back on his horse. And he headed out.

"We should go search too," Cassie was saying.

Okay. At least he wouldn't have to attempt to get off the horse and look embarrassingly weird, Oliver thought. But he wasn't really enjoying being on the horse, either. Breathe in, breathe out, he told himself. The horse started picking up speed again, as Cassie tried to follow Thomas Jefferson. But he had disappeared too.

They found themselves venturing into a wooded area. How would they ever find her? Oliver wondered. He had no idea where they were. And neither, he assumed, did Cassie. But she kept on urging the horse forward, while calling Ruby's name.

Oliver joined in. "Ruby!" he screamed. "Patsy! Where are you?" His worries were increasing. His stomach was hurting again. Where was she? He thought about his parents. What they would say when they learned that he and Cassie couldn't find Ruby, and that she was in another century. Would the hat be able to get them back? Or was it done with Oliver entirely? Would Sam help him out if need be?

"Ruby!" Cassie was shouting. "Where are you? Patsy Jefferson! Where are you?"

And where had Thomas Jefferson gone, for that matter? He had completely vanished.

They had entered a clearing in the forest. The trees reached high above them. Oliver had almost forgotten how hot he was, but all of a sudden it hit him. "Water?" he inquired of Cassie.

"I don't have any water, Oliver," she snapped at him, pulling the horse's reins. It stopped. "I wish I did, but I guess we didn't think of that when we stopped back at our house, did we?"

She seemed really stressed out, Oliver thought. She didn't usually snap at him. She twisted her hands around. "What are we going to do?" she said. "I keep thinking of all these awful things that could have . . . ," and she trailed off.

Oliver did too. Capture? Prison? Worse?

"Well, all we can do is keep looking," Cassie said, and they started moving forward again, back into the trees.

"Ruby!" Oliver called. "Patsy!"

"Olls?" came a voice.

"Ruby?" Oliver and Cassie said together. Oliver noticed Cassie's voice was shaking again. His own probably was too.

"Over here!" Ruby said. It definitely was Ruby. Oliver took a huge breath, and felt . . . felt . . . could it be? Happiness? About Ruby? Well, stranger things had happened. Although maybe not to him.

"Is that your sister and brother?" came another voice. "You said they would find us, and here they are!"

Cassie guided the horse toward the sound of the voices. And there was Ruby, sitting with Patsy Jefferson on a fallen log! Cassie jumped off the horse and ran over to hug Ruby. Oliver found himself doing the same. They both hugged Patsy Jefferson too.

"I'm so mad at you, but I'm just so glad you're okay," Cassie said, hugging Ruby again. "Why did you just run off like that?"

"Olls, you were actually on a horse?" Ruby said, clearly changing the subject. She smiled at him. "Miracle of miracles. So I think I broke my ankle. Or maybe sprained it. That's why we're sitting here on the log."

"What?" Cassie said. "How . . ."

"Ruby got into our carriage," Patsy Jefferson said, seeming eager to participate in the conversation. "We had the most interesting talk about girls and women and what they could contribute to our society. And then when we arrived at this other house, where we were to take shelter, Ruby and I decided to go for a walk, so we could keep talking."

They had walked into the woods, and Ruby had been so involved in writing things down in her notebook that she had tripped over a log and ended up badly twisting her ankle.

"See?" she said, pointing at her right ankle. It did look swollen. "I can't really put any weight on it," she continued. "And we had no way to let anyone know where we were. I didn't want to send Patsy back to the house herself, you know, since we weren't sure if the British had figured out where the Jeffersons had gone. It's a real pain that I can't use my . . ."

Cell phone? Oliver wondered. But at least Ruby hadn't said it. It would have completely confused Patsy Jefferson.

"Let's get you on the horse," Cassie said. "The three of us can walk. Do you know the way back to the house?"

"Jeez, I have no idea," Ruby said, as Cassie and Oliver boosted her onto the horse. "Ow!" she cried out.

"I know how to get back," Patsy piped up. "Ruby was busy writing things in her notebook, but I was paying attention. We need to go that way," and she pointed to the left and then paused for a moment, a worried look on her face. "Where's Pappa?"

"He's somewhere in the woods, searching for you guys," Oliver said, as the group started out in the direction Patsy had indicated.

"So he escaped the British?" Patsy said. "Oh, how wonderful!" And she clasped her hands together.

It was much slower getting back to the house than it had been in the other direction, because they were walking. Well, except Ruby. And nobody was saying much. It was still incredibly hot, and Oliver kept being tempted to lift the hat off his head and wipe his brow. But he didn't.

Finally, they came in sight of the house. "You see?

There it is!" Patsy said excitedly. "And there are Mamma and Pappa and Polly!"

Sure enough, the three other Jeffersons were outside the house.

"Pappa! Mamma! Polly!" Patsy yelled, and she ran ahead to meet them. As the Jeffersons all embraced one another, Patsy was obviously telling them about Ruby and what had happened.

Mrs. Jefferson hastened toward them.

"We should take you to a doctor, but with the British . . ." She leaned over to inspect Ruby's ankle. "Perhaps you could just remain in a chair with your foot wrapped up?"

"Perhaps," Ruby said. "But perhaps, Olls, you know . . . ," and she looked at Oliver. And at the hat.

Clearly, twenty-first-century medicine was an improvement over the eighteenth-century version. "Yeah, okay," Oliver said. He wanted to stay here. He had a lot more questions to ask Thomas Jefferson. About the Hemings family. About how Thomas Jefferson could keep his children as his slaves. Thomas Jefferson had promised Oliver and Cassie he'd discuss the whole Declaration of Independence thing with them. And Oliver knew Cassie wanted to ask him about UVA.

But he really should get Ruby back home. He glanced once more at Thomas Jefferson, who was busy listening to something Patsy was saying. And Oliver took off the hat.

A second later, he, Cassie, and Ruby—and the hat—were back at home, just inside the front door of their house.

"Ruby?" His mom hurried in from the kitchen, looking perplexed. "How did you get home?"

Ruby exchanged glances with Cassie and Oliver. "Magic," she said. And she smirked.

"Very funny," their mom said, frowning. "I assume your friend's parents drove you?"

"Yeah," Cassie said quickly. "They drove her home."

"And how did the project go?" asked their dad, who had appeared behind their mom.

"Project? Oh, really well," Ruby said. "But I just twisted my ankle, and I can't put any weight on it." She showed her ankle to their parents.

"Oh, no!" their mom said. "It's awfully swollen. We should go to the emergency room right now! It might be broken!"

Amid all the commotion—Ruby and their mom departed for the hospital and Cassie started discussing the school play auditions with their dad—Oliver slipped away. He went into his room with the hat and closed the door.

"So," he said to the hat.

"So," the hat replied.

"What's next?" Oliver asked. But somehow he knew. The hat had said a week or so, and it had been a week and two days. And the hat really belonged to Sam.

"My dear Oliver," the hat said in its squeaky voice. "We have had a wonderful week, have we not?"

Oliver thought about it. Meeting Thomas Jefferson. Meeting Madison Hemings. Meeting Mrs. Jefferson and Patsy and Polly. And everything that had happened in his real life. The possibility of getting his black belt. The arrival of Colin and Rhiannon. Getting to work on the science fair project with Colin and Rhiannon and Katie.

And, of course, rescuing Ruby. It really wouldn't have been so great to have her stuck in the eighteenth century forever, would it?

"We have," Oliver replied. "But I know, you need to go back to Sam now, right?"

"Correct," the hat said. "Keep in mind, however, that if I have been willing to be lent once, perhaps I will be again. And adventures can be shared. Now please put me back in my bag. I am awfully tired."

Oliver did. And as he lay down on his bed and breathed in and out, deeply, a feeling of what he could only describe as hopefulness stole over him. It really didn't matter if Cassie had the social skills and Ruby had the sports skills, did it? He had his own skills, right? Or so it seemed at this moment. And he told himself that everything would be okay.

Acknowledgments
and Author's Note

Many thanks to everyone who helped me as I worked on this book. There are more people than I can name here, including wonderful friends who read and commented on the manuscript, but I particularly wanted to thank my parents, Marvin Kalb and Madeleine Kalb, writers themselves, who have supported my writing efforts for many decades now, and my husband and son, David Levitt and Aaron Kalb Levitt, who traveled with me to Monticello and generously put up with my weird writing hours. Much love to you all.

Many thanks to everyone at Schiffer, including Pete Schiffer, Tracee Groff, Kim Grandizio, Carey Massimini, Jamie Elfrank, Harrison Lutz, Cheryl Weber, and many others; this is our third partnership and I am incredibly appreciative.

Finally, a huge thank-you to Rob Lunsford, artist extraordinaire, without whom this book would be a shadow of itself. It's been a privilege to work with you!

A note on sources: I read many books—both for adults and for kids—and consulted many websites as I researched and wrote this book. Some of the most useful books were *Thomas Jefferson: The Art of Power*, by Jon Meacham; *The Hemingses of Monticello: An American Family*, by Annette Gordon-Reed; *Thomas Jefferson: An Intimate History*, by Fawn M. Brodie; and *"Those Who Labor for My Happiness": Slavery at Thomas Jefferson's Monticello*, by Lucia Stanton. The most informative website was Monticello's own website. That's where I got the story of James Madison visiting Thomas Jefferson to watch the 1811 eclipse.

About the Author

Deborah Kalb is a freelance writer and editor who spent more than twenty years working as a journalist. She is the coauthor, with her father, Marvin Kalb, of *Haunting Legacy: Vietnam and the American Presidency from Ford to Obama* and has always been interested in presidents and history. She lives with her family in the Washington, DC, area.

About the Illustrator

Robert Lunsford has been a graphic artist/illustrator for nearly forty years. A graduate of Virginia Commonwealth University's School of the Arts, Rob spent his career as a graphic artist for his hometown daily newspaper, the *Roanoke Times*. Rob is known for his ability to tell stories through pictures and information graphics and is recognized by the Virginia Press Association, Society of News Design, and American Advertising Federation. A founding member and tuba/saxophone player in Roanoke's Norman Fishing Tackle Choir marching band, Rob enjoys woodworking, music, building things, and making pictures. He is married to a fellow artist and elementary school teacher and has two grown children.